Michael Underwood and The Murder Room

>>> This title is part of The Murder Room, our series dedicated to making available out-of-print or hard-to-find titles by classic crime writers.

Crime fiction has always held up a mirror to society. The Victorians were fascinated by sensational murder and the emerging science of detection; now we are obsessed with the forensic detail of violent death. And no other genre has so captivated and enthralled readers.

Vast troves of classic crime writing have for a long time been unavailable to all but the most dedicated frequenters of second-hand bookshops. The advent of digital publishing means that we are now able to bring you the backlists of a huge range of titles by classic and contemporary crime writers, some of which have been out of print for decades.

From the genteel amateur private eyes of the Golden Age and the femmes fatales of pulp fiction, to the morally ambiguous hard-boiled detectives of mid twentieth-century America and their descendants who walk our twenty-first century streets, The Murder Room has it all. **>>>**

The Murder Room
Where Criminal Minds Meet

themurderroom.com

Michael Underwood (1916–1992)

Michael Underwood (the pseudonym of John Michael Evelyn) was born in Worthing, Sussex and educated at Christ Church College, Oxford. He was called to the Bar in 1939 and served in the British army during World War Two. He returned to work in the Department of Public Prosecutions until his retirement in 1976, and wrote almost 50 crime novels informed by his career in the law. His five series characters include Sergeant Nick Atwell and lawyer Rosa Epton, of whom is was said by the *Washington Post* that she 'outdoes Perry Mason'.

Standalone titles

A Crime Apart

Shem's Demise

The Silent Liars

Anything But the Truth

Smooth Justice

Victim of Circumstance

A Clear Case of Suicide

The Hand of Fate

The Shadow Game

Michael Underwood

An Orion book

Copyright © Isobel Mackenzie 1969

The right of Michael Underwood to be identified as the author of this work has been asserted in accordance with the Copyright, Designs and Patents Act 1988.

This edition published by
The Orion Publishing Group Ltd
Orion House
5 Upper St Martin's Lane
London WC2H 9EA

An Hachette UK company
A CIP catalogue record for this book is available from the British Library

ISBN 978 1 4719 0790 6

www.orionbooks.co.uk

To Tim and Suzy

CHAPTER ONE

Hotel lobbies, seldom the cosiest of places, manage to have a bleak cheerfulness all of their own at half past six in the morning. Or so it seemed to Martin Ainsworth on the mercifully few occasions he found himself in one at that hour. They are filled with smells, all stale, which seem to reflect the mood of the night staff waiting with sullen inertia to go off duty. Electric cables criss-cross the floor and wrap themselves round the feet of the departing guest as he tries to sidestep the cleaners, heading, laden with his own baggage, towards the receipt of custom.

Martin was travelling light (a single small suitcase) and so was nimbly able to avoid the coil of flex which tried to lasso his right ankle as he stepped from the lift and walked across to pay his bill.

A stout man with a florid complexion, who was perspiring freely even at this hour of the morning, was laboriously counting out ten-mark notes under the contemptuous gaze of the night cashier who gave the impression of hoping that the bill could not be met and the police could be sent for. Eventually, however, the florid-faced man let out a slight grunt and pushed across a pile of notes. The clerk counted them with almost insolent deliberation before reluctantly receipting the bill and turning his attention to Martin.

'Room 237,' Martin said.

The clerk fetched the bill from a portfolio on the desk behind him.

'Herr Ainsworth?' he queried.

'Correct.'

'You just arrived last night?' he asked with a faint frown.

Martin nodded. 'About half past ten.'

'You leave Munich again so soon?'

'I'm afraid so.'

'Have a good trip,' he said, baring his teeth in what Martin charitably assumed to be a smile.

'Thanks.'

This was more than he had wished the previous departing

1

guest and Martin began to wonder why he had been singled out for special treatment. But he quickly checked himself. If he allowed a few perfunctory words from a hotel clerk to set his imagination going, he would work himself into a state of neurosis before his journey proper had ever started.

'Any chance of finding a taxi at this hour?' he asked.

The clerk shrugged indifferently. 'It is early,' he said through a smothered yawn, and turned away. His interest in Martin had clearly been nothing more than a formality and even that had now evaporated.

Picking up his bag, Martin walked across the lobby and stepped out into the thin sunshine of a May morning.

A tram trundled past, making the noise which he had associated with Munich trams ever since his student days in the city. He saw one approaching from the opposite direction with 'Hauptbahnhof' on its headboard and he crossed the street to join the queue of workers waiting at the halt sign. Half of them were foreigners and it occurred to him, not for the first time, how topsy-turvy had become the economies of countries which had to import labour from others whose own economies were in a state of even worse malfunction.

He managed to squeeze on to the rear platform of the tram, where he found himself wedged between a Greek and an Arab. At least, that was his guess as to their nationality. They eyed him with considerable interest, as well they might, seeing that middle-aged 'city gentlemen' in rather obviously casual attire were an unusual sight on their morning ride to work.

Martin had given a good deal of thought to what he should wear and was dressed in a dark blue terylene and linen jacket, a black woollen T-shirt, which he reckoned would look no scruffier at the end of the journey than it did at the beginning, a pair of charcoal grey slacks, which already looked as though he had slept several nights in them, and his suede desert boots which he had selected as being the most suitable footwear for all eventualities ahead.

'By the way,' Peacock had said to him at one of the final briefing sessions in London, 'I suggest you wear something comfortable on your feet. Something you can run in and, if necessary, effectively kick with.'

Well, he could certainly run all right in his desert boots, though he was less sure of their kicking properties. Perhaps he would have done better to have worn an old pair of climbing boots. The trouble was that no one had been able to give him

2

any idea of the ratio of running to kicking; and, after all, everything depended on that. He hoped very much there would be none of either. Peacock had been entirely optimistic on that score, but then it had been in Peacock's interest to radiate confident optimism.

The tram came to a juddering halt outside the huge main station and Martin got out.

For several seconds he just stood staring at the wide façade, as much for reasons of nostalgia as of putting off the moment of irrevocable surrender to the devious Peacock's elaborate plans. People in Peacock's line of business were, of course, required to be devious beneath their bland, but always wary, exteriors.

But Peacock was not in Martin's immediate thoughts and his mind had slipped back thirty-odd short years to the misty autumn evening when he had arrived at this station, a boy straight from school, to study at the university. Hitler had recently come to power and Martin had emerged from the station feeling tired and faintly homesick after his long journey to find himself caught up in a parade of S.A. He could see them now, their brown shirts and swastika armbands and their self-important expressions, as they marched towards Karlsplatz.

There were tall and short, thin and tubby, bank clerks and office managers, dentists and engineers, but all with the same air of stern dedication. Cries of 'Heil Hitler' greeted their progress along the street as bystanders thrust out right arms in salute. Some saluted with less fervour than others. And some did not salute at all.

Martin could still recall his feeling of faint chill as he watched the parade pass. It had been nothing more than an undefined shiver of apprehension, an awareness that 'fun' had no part in the Nazi vocabulary. For those who could read, the writing was already on the wall, though not even the benefit of hindsight could persuade Martin that he had been one of them. But eighteen-year-olds were less politically sophisticated and articulate in those days, he reflected.

And now here he was, over thirty years later, standing not more than fifty yards from the spot where he had witnessed that parade—the first of many he was to see in the year which followed.

One thing for sure, if it had not been for Hitler and all his works, he would not now be standing outside Munich Station, suitcase in hand and mind filled with uneasiness. If the distant past had brought its own measure of menace, so suddenly had the immediate future.

Bracing himself, he crossed the road and made his way round to the side of the station. As he turned a corner, he saw a bright yellow bus parked in a bay about fifty yards away. There were a number of people standing around it and stepping over one another's suitcases. When he got closer, he could read the black letters on the side of the bus, 'HEROLD TOURING A.G.', and knew that this was to be his home for the next three days. A bit closer still and he could see the slotted board beside the door of the bus which read 'MÜNCHEN–ISTANBUL'.

This was the bus all right and he found himself automatically casting curious glances at his fellow passengers, until he remembered Peacock's strict injunction.

'Behave quite naturally all the time. In particular, don't stare at people as if you were directing a laser beam at them. Nothing draws attention to you more quickly than that.'

At any other time, the route board would have given him a delicious thrill. As it was, however, he saw it only as a signpost to nemesis.

An unshaven official of Herold Touring A.G. in a shiny suit with bulging pockets was standing by the entrance to the bus, holding a large sheet of paper on which he made ticks with a blunt pencil as passengers reported to him.

'Gursan,' Martin heard the man ahead of him say. He was short and powerfully built, with an expanse of forehead, a bushy black moustache and a pair of blue eyes which seemed to find the world an amusing place to be in.

'Seat 17,' the official announced after consulting his list and Mr Gursan, who had been smiling at everyone within sight, stepped into the bus.

'Ainsworth,' Martin said, keeping his voice self-consciously low, though no one appeared to be paying him any particular attention.

'Seat 38. At back,' the official said without looking up.

'What do I do with my bag?'

'Leave over here please.' He nodded towards the rear of the bus where the driver and co-driver were loading the baggage trailer which resembled a large yellow oven on wheels. The two drivers could hardly have been more different in appearance. One, who looked around thirty, was tall and thin, with a

4

head of thick blond hair. His nordic origins were unmistakable. The other, who hopped energetically in and out of the trailer, was short and dark and seemed to be made of rubber. He also gave the impression of being indestructibly cheerful as he kept up a non-stop flow of quips in a variety of different languages for the benefit of the small audience which had gathered to watch the loading operations.

'Sind Sie Deutsch?' he asked, seizing Martin's case from him.

'Nein, Englisch.'

'Oh, fine stuff. Jolly old England. I once live six months in Birmingham.'

'What were you doing there?' Martin inquired with a smile.

'What I was not doing! I was doing everything. Very fine place Birmingham.'

'Where do you come from? You're not German, are you?'

'I am Persian, but I have German wife and many fine babies. My wife is blonde like Hans.' He grinned at his fellow driver before disappearing inside the trailer with Martin's case. Hans, who had been waiting for their conversation to finish, gave a helpless shrug.

'Verrückt!' he muttered.

'Who's saying me crazy?' the Persian asked, popping out again. 'Poor Hans, he can't speak good English, but he's fine driver. Aren't you, Hans?'

He gave the German's cheek a friendly pat and quickly ducked out of range as the other aimed a lazy cuff in his direction and said, 'Du bist wirklich verrückt, Ali.'

Martin decided it was time to go and find his seat. As he walked down the aisle of the bus, he received an amused wink from Mr Gursan who was sitting with hands clasped across his stomach, an expression of hopeful interest on his face. Martin acknowledged the wink with a smile. Mr Gursan had a strongly dependable look and, if the opportunity presented itself naturally, he decided he would try and find out something about him. He might prove a valuable ally. But even as the thought entered his mind, it conjured up a frowning Peacock.

'Don't fraternise with the other passengers,' he had said. 'It could be dangerous. Exchange the usual travellers' banalities if you must, but don't go further than that. For heaven's sake don't go probing the life histories of any of them or anything of that sort! You don't need to know where they live, or what they do when they're at home. If they tell you things about themselves, that's their look-out, but no inquisitive questions please.' He had grinned. 'The English are the one people who can get away with reserve without rousing suspicion, which can be very useful at times.'

Martin had pointed out that, in his vocabulary, travellers' banalities often included an exchange of information of a personal nature. 'Not in mine, they don't,' Peacock had said firmly.

Seat 38 turned out to be two rows from the back and right over the rear wheels, he observed with dismay. It was the aisle seat with number 37, still unoccupied, on its inside.

He sat down and waited. Waited, conscious of his beating heart, for the journey to start; but, above all, he was waiting for the occupant of the seat next to him to arrive and claim her place...

Trying to appear relaxed, he gazed at the dozen or so people still standing around outside the bus and wondered which was Peacock's local man come to see and report back that he had safely reached the starting point. He could not believe that Peacock would not check on that.

He glanced at his watch and saw that it was three minutes before half past seven. The bus was now nearly three-quarters full and there was an air of impending departure.

The tall driver, Hans, had put on his jacket and was running a comb through his hair. Ali was still playing the comedian to a small group idling their time away until the bus left. There were three long-haired youths and two girls, and an old man of the sort that frequents the public galleries of Magistrates' Courts in England. Once the bus departed, they would presumably drift away in search of further free distraction.

Martin noticed a taxi pull up about thirty yards away and a girl jump out in an obvious hurry. She paid off the driver and came half-running in the direction of the bus. She had very fair hair and was wearing a tightly belted white mackintosh with upturned collar. This, he felt sure, must be the girl whose fate was to be linked with his own over the next few days. This was the girl about whom Peacock had told him so much—and, at the same time, about whom he knew nothing at all.

At the last minute, she veered away and disappeared through one of the side entrances to the Station, leaving Martin feeling as he often had on the tennis court after racing back to retrieve a lob only to see it drop out.

He glanced again at his watch. It was now one minute before the half hour and both drivers were standing by the entrance talking to the official with the list. A stewardess in a dark mustard-coloured uniform was standing at the end of the aisle counting the passengers.

The official with the list looked across impatiently to where a number of passengers were dismounting from a tram. Peacock's man, if he had ever been there, must now have taken himself off. At least, there was no one left in the vicinity who was showing the slightest interest in the bus.

Martin fell to wondering what he would do if the bus started with the seat beside him still unoccupied. This was one contingency which had not been covered in any of his briefing sessions with Peacock. It took him only a second's reflection, however, to realise that there was nothing he could do but sit tight. But it would be disconcerting to say the least. Rather like steeling oneself for the surgeon's knife, only to be told when already in the theatre that the doctors are not sure it will be necessary to operate after all.

There was a sudden flurry of movement by the entrance and the stewardess stepped aside to let someone enter.

Martin almost ricked his neck in his determination not to stare at the girl who was coming towards him. He was vaguely aware of a pale, tense face, a pair of opaque dark glasses which completely hid her eyes and slightly wind-blown, shoulder-length hair. He had nearly jumped up from his seat before she ever reached him, but had realised just in time what a give-away this would be to unfriendly eyes.

She was now standing over him.

'Bitte, Entschuldigung,' she murmured, as he got up to let her into her seat. She slipped past him without a glance and sat down and at once lit a cigarette.

So this was Anna Schmidt...

CHAPTER TWO

It had been just over two weeks before that the man named Peacock had erupted into Martin Ainsworth's life.

What had happened was this. Martin had been due to spend the latter half of May and most of June out in the Persian

Gulf where he had been briefed by one of the big oil companies to appear in an arbitration case. In view of this, John, his Chambers' head clerk, had spent hours on the telephone rearranging things so that he would have to return only the minimum number of briefs and had finally achieved the impossible, as only barristers' clerks can in such circumstances, when a cable came through announcing the postponement of the arbitration hearing until the autumn. As far as Martin ever gathered, the postponement was due to the whim of a local ruler, but the result was that he suddenly found himself with six relatively slack weeks ahead of him.

He told his clerk to give him a couple of weeks free, the sudden void in his professional life having given him an unforeseen urge to take a short holiday, and had promised that he would then return and be ready to deal with such work as the clerk had managed to redirect on to his table.

It was at this moment that Peacock had entered the scene and Martin had since been left to speculate as to the degree to which his emergence from the shadows had been fortuitous. Though he had never admitted it, Martin had a sneaking belief that Peacock had somehow learnt that a normally busy barrister suddenly had time on his hands. Otherwise, it was really too much of a coincidence.

It all began on a Thursday evening about five o'clock. Martin was standing in the window of his room in Chambers observing the progress of a couple of girls in mini-skirts and thinking, not without a certain amount of relish, of the outraged reaction of a few of the stuffier old judges who had been on the Bench when he had first begun practising at the Bar. He hoped they were looking down over the edge of their celestial clouds and might even fall off in a spasm of choleric affront. Personally, he found the particular girls extremely attractive and he moved towards one side of the window the better to keep them in view.

He was still gazing at them when the door opened and John stuck his head round.

'There's a Mr Peacock on the telephone, sir. He says it's personal and private and rather urgent.' John had never trusted the Chambers' switchboard since an embarrassing occasion when a caller had heard himself described as 'Sounding like a peevish sheep' and had let it be icily known that he didn't much care for the description. Since then, on the occasions when there was no one else to take calls (normally

Edward, the junior clerk, or Maureen, the typist, did so) he had made it a rule to leave the switchboard and personally convey his impressions of those callers who might be anything from cabinet ministers to well-spoken lunatics. 'He *sounds* all right, shall I put him through?'

'No clues at all as to who he is?'

'None. I thought perhaps the name might mean something to you, sir.'

'It doesn't, I'm afraid. However, I'd better speak to him.'

A minute later, a faintly drawling voice came on the line.

'Mr Ainsworth?'

'Speaking.'

'My name's Peacock. We've never met, but I believe you know a colleague of mine called Noyce.'

'Noyce?' Martin repeated, trying unsuccessfully to recall the name.

'Yes. In Berlin a few years ago.'

'A-ah!' Martin exclaimed as a flood of memories, mostly disagreeable, were suddenly released in his mind.

Peacock, however, chose to ignore the note of wariness that had entered his voice.

'I should very much like to have the opportunity of meeting you. I think we also have a common acquaintance in Oliver Whyte, whom I was talking to yesterday. Could you manage lunch one day fairly soon?'

'Yes, I think I could,' Martin replied cautiously.

'That's fine. Is tomorrow too soon?'

'No, I could manage tomorrow.'

'Would the Ritz suit you? I know it's a bit staid, but it's one of the few places you can eat without getting splashed by people spooning up their soup at the next table. At most restaurants these days you almost sit in some stranger's lap. Well, see you tomorrow at one o'clock. I'll book a table and wait for you in the dining-room.'

He rang off without waiting for any response, leaving Martin staring abstractedly out of the window. Not even a brigade of mini-skirted girls would have attracted his attention at that moment.

So Peacock was a colleague of Noyce! Noyce who had been the head of one of the numerous intelligence agencies in Berlin when Martin had made his first—and, as he had subsequently vowed, last—foray into the world of espionage. And a pretty disastrous foray it had been! A humiliating fiasco which he preferred not to remember.

An hour later, he arrived back at his flat in Knightsbridge to find all the lights on and Aunt Virginia, reclining feet up on the sofa, buried in a travel brochure. She was a small bird-like woman who showed little evidence of her seventy-five years, in which respect she had been greatly assisted by a life of wealthy ease. She had been widowed twenty years previously and for the past fifteen she and Martin had shared an extremely comfortable flat to the convenience and pleasure of each of them. They lived their separate lives, but enjoyed a bond of mutual respect and affection.

'What do you think Barbados would be like in October?' she inquired, after he had poured himself a Scotch and mixed her a Dry Martini.

'Apart from hurricanes, you mean?'

'I thought it was a bit early,' she said, turning a page of the brochure. 'What about a safari in East Africa?'

'For yourself?' he asked in surprise.

'Why not?'

'I didn't know you were particularly interested in wild animals.'

'I'm not sure that I am, but I feel it might be an experience.'

'Cheaper to spend a few days at the zoo.'

'Lots of women my age go on safari these days,' she replied with spirit.

'I don't believe it. You'll be telling me next that you were considering Barbados for the skin-diving. Anyway, what is that brochure you're looking at?'

'It came through the letter-box this afternoon. It's called "Sterling Holidays in the Sterling Area".'

'Presumably only intended for those with oodles of sterling,' Martin commented.

Aunt Virginia laid the brochure down and looked at her watch. 'I'm dining and playing bridge at Marcia's this evening. What'll you do about dinner?'

'I'll forage in the larder. I'm not particularly hungry.'

'I don't think Mrs Carp has left anything either. For some silly reason I had it in my head you weren't coming in this evening.'

Mrs Carp was the daily woman who not only kept the flat clean but who did a certain amount of cooking when Aunt Virginia, a first-class cook, was feeling lazy or otherwise disinclined to spend time in the kitchen.

10

'Don't fuss, I'll be all right.'

In fact, largely because it was not a regular occurrence in his life, Martin rather enjoyed foraging in the larder and cooking a meal for himself. Fried eggs invariably found a place on his menu even though the resultant smell and mess were out of all proportion to such simple fare. Nevertheless, he would sit down afterwards with his cup of instant coffee, feeling as satisfied as if he had climbed the Matterhorn or won the men's singles at Wimbledon.

But on this particular evening, he found his after-dinner thoughts focused entirely on his forthcoming lunch with Peacock. He could think of only one reason why Peacock should want to see him and that was to enlist his aid, which was not a welcome prospect. However, he would not prejudge their meeting and would go to the Ritz with as open a mind as the Edwardian dandies who once paraded their plumage within its purlieus.

It was exactly half a minute after one o'clock when he entered the dining-room the next day. He had barely paused to glance around before he was aware of a tall, sandy-haired man with a slight stoop getting up from a table over in one corner and coming towards him with a tentative smile on his lean face.

'Mr Ainsworth? I thought it must be you from the description I had. We're over in the corner.' They reached the table and sat down. 'Let me order you a drink?'

'I'll have a Tio Pepé.'

'Yes,' Peacock went on. 'Oliver Whyte described you very accurately. I gather you and he still play a certain amount of tennis together.'

Martin and Oliver Whyte had been at Oxford together and had gained lawn tennis blues the same year. Whyte had gone into the Diplomatic Service straight from university and the two men had since kept in touch with one another, even though contact was at times only maintained by an exchange of Christmas cards when Whyte was in a post abroad. He was currently back at the Foreign Office and Martin had seen him fairly often over the past twelve months, usually, as Peacock had correctly gathered, on a tennis court. They were both members of Queens and played all the year round.

'As a matter of fact I have a letter of introduction from him. Perhaps you'd better read it, since it establishes my bona fides.'

He pulled an envelope from an inside pocket of his jacket

and handed it to Martin, who saw that it was addressed to him in Oliver Whyte's neat classical hand.

He opened it and took out the short note on Foreign Office headed paper which read:

'Dear Martin,

This introduces Guy Peacock of our Service who has something to discuss with you. I know that he hopes very much you'll be able to help him:

We must have some more tennis soon. Indeed, once I've recovered from a humiliating, though mercifully mild, attack of gout.

Yours,
Oliver.'

Martin looked up from reading the note to find Peacock watching him. He had cool green eyes whose colour was emphasised by the ginger of his eyebrows. His mouth was small and could, Martin surmised, quickly reflect silent anger.

'O.K.?' Peacock inquired with a faint smile. 'Am I vouched for? Actually, Oliver and I are not engaged on the same work, as you may have gathered. Oliver is the real thing, whereas I only masquerade as a diplomat, but our paths happen to cross quite often.'

'I understand Oliver is in line for an ambassadorship,' Martin said.

'He'll get one very shortly, I hear.' Peacock who had been fingering the edge of his menu now picked it up and said, 'Shall we get the ordering done with? I imagine you're filled with a fair amount of curiosity about this meeting and I'm not one who holds back from talking business until the coffee stage. Now, what would you like to start with...?'

Peacock ordered their meal with the deliberation which the prospect of good food demands, taking particular care in the choice of wine after a short consultation with Martin on the rival merits of a Moselle or a Hock to start with.

As soon as the wine waiter had departed and a lower minion had gathered up most of the cutlery and then replaced it, Martin leant forward and, in a tone which he tried to keep light, asked, 'In what way are you hoping I'll help you?'

Peacock pursed his lips in faint annoyance as though he did not care for having the initiative wrested from him quite so crudely.

'By taking a bus ride,' he said, after a second's pause, giving Martin an amused smile which seemed to say, 'You'd better let me tell it my way, hadn't you?' 'A bus ride from Munich to Istanbul to be exact,' he went on. 'But let me start in the right place.' He twiddled the signet ring on his little finger, as though tuning in his thoughts before continuing. 'We have an agent in East Germany whom we wish to get out. I needn't tell you anything about her—yes, it's a girl by the way—because the rescue operation doesn't require you to know any of her personal details. Indeed, it doesn't require you to do anything but sit on the bus and enjoy the scenery. We've devised a very simple plan and it's this. At a given point along the route—in fact, when you're passing through Bulgaria—this girl we're going to get out will take the place of the one who has been sitting in the seat beside you from Munich. The only thing you will be required to do is to pretend, if necessary, that it is the same girl all the way through. The odds are that it won't be necessary and that you will have a trouble-free run.' He searched Martin's face for some glimmer of reaction, but saw only an expression of suspended judgment. 'Let me answer one or two of the more obvious questions that have come to your mind. In the first place, the girl who will be in the seat next to you from Munich, does, of course, bear a very marked physical resemblance to the one who is to be rescued. That's an essential part of the whole plan. Next, you don't need to worry about what happens to the first girl after the exchange has taken place. That's all taken care of and it's not a part of the operation which affects you. As I know you appreciate, an operation of this sort involves a large number of human cogs and "the need to know" is the over-riding principle. No one cog is given more information than he needs to mesh with those either side of him.'

Martin nodded. 'So I take a bus from Munich to Istanbul and dare the world to suggest that I've got a different girl sitting next to me at the end of the ride. Is that really all there is to it?'

'That's it exactly,' Peacock said in a satisfied tone.

'When?'

'In about a couple of weeks' time.'

'And how long will it take?'

'It's a three-day bus ride. Add on two days for flying to Munich and back from Istanbul and the whole thing can be done comfortably inside of a week.' He smiled as he added,

'And all expenses paid, of course. You can spend a few extra days in Istanbul if you like. If you're not pressed for time, that is. Indeed, I'd suggest you should if you've never been there. It's a fascinating city and we could certainly wangle you a bit of extra money to cover that.'

'I once spent a few hectic hours there on a cruise and have always intended going back some time,' Martin said reflectively.

'There you are then! A chance to explore it at leisure at H.M.G.'s expense!'

Conversation ceased while their waiter brought the next course. Martin had ordered a veal chop garnished with button mushrooms and Peacock was having Steak Tartare. It seemed to Martin rather appropriate food for one who dwelt in a ruthless world of sophisticated gangsterism. Raw meat!

'Do you feel able to give me an answer yet?' Peacock asked, after the waiter had departed. 'There's obviously a good deal more to tell you if you're going to agree to help us. On the other hand, I think I've probably told you sufficient to enable you to make up your mind. What about it?'

'You've made it sound all rather hum-drum and plain sailing, but I imagine a good many things can go wrong in this sort of operation. I think I'm entitled to know what the risks are before giving you an answer.'

'Ye-es,' Peacock said thoughtfully. 'Things can, of course, go wrong—badly wrong. But even if some link in the plan does break, I can't see that it will involve you. You're going to know nothing about either of the two girls and nobody is going to be able to connect you in any way with either of them. You just happen to be in the next seat ...'

'But it's going to look highly suspicious—and that's an understatement for a start—if every other passenger on the bus swears that a swap has taken place and that the girl next to me at the end of the journey is definitely not the one who started in that seat.'

'I assure you that won't happen,' Peacock said emphatically. 'I ask you to accept my word for that.' He went on after a pause, 'But it is possible that if something goes wrong you might find yourself being questioned by local police, together, that is, with all your fellow passengers. It's then you stick to your story and I promise you that you won't be able to be caught out.'

'What are these girls?' Martin asked. 'Identical twins?'

14

Peacock did not answer. His green eyes, moreover, were as inexpressive as a cat's, and Martin knew he was not going to receive a reply to his question.

'Supposing I am questioned and supposing it's suggested that I'm a British spy?'

'You deny it. You're not one and there'll be no evidence that you're in any way connected with either of the girls. You're just an English tourist taking an interesting trip.'

'But that won't prevent someone's security service grabbing me and holding me in prison, if they're so minded.'

'If you run into really serious trouble, you'll have various phone numbers to ring and people you can contact along the way.'

'A fat lot of good that'll do me if I'm lodged in a Bulgarian jail!'

'Look, Mr Ainsworth,' Peacock said with a sigh. 'Life is full of risks. I'm not trying to say there aren't any risks in this assignment. What I do say, however, is that you're less likely to find yourself in a Bulgarian jail than you are to be run over by a number 9 bus as you walk out of this hotel.

'My expectation is that you won't even be called upon to undertake the small bit of bluff I've mentioned. Nevertheless, if you agree to help, you'll certainly be fully briefed on every foreseeable eventuality. So, what about it?'

'Just one more question before I give you my answer. How did you come to pick on me?'

Peacock made a small deprecating gesture with one hand. 'You know something about our work from that time in Berlin, you speak reasonable German, you take slightly off-beat holidays. In a word, you have the perfect cover for the job. Moreover, you're not identified with any of our regulars. That was the snag about the first chap we had in mind. His professional status in the field could have proved a liability. Frankly, I'm much happier at the thought of someone such as yourself playing this particular part.'

'What happened to your first choice?' Martin inquired. 'One of the other side put a bullet through him?'

Peacock threw back his head and let out a laugh.

'If you really want to know, he's caught chicken-pox from his ten-year-old daughter. Though I'm not sure that he wouldn't have preferred a bullet, his wife says he's smothered with spots and feeling extremely sorry for himself.'

There followed a pause during which Martin gazed out of a

window at London's new jagged skyline on the far side of Green Park. It gave the unhappy appearance of a lower jaw of uneven and missing teeth.

'Yes,' he said at length, 'all right, I'll take your bus ride.'

In the two weeks which followed, Martin attended a number of briefing sessions with Peacock, at some of which they were joined by certain of Peacock's colleagues who were specialists in various fields of intelligence activity.

These meetings all took place in Peacock's office in a government building of inappropriately innocent appearance and designation. Martin used to gaze round at the unmistakable ministry furniture and trappings and wonder whether Peacock, a man who controlled agents on the other side of the iron curtain, who despatched people on dangerous missions and who wrote off failure in terms of human lives, had as much difficulty in getting a new chair or side table as would a sub-collector of taxes in Droitwich. He imagined it probably was so. If your office was not a public show-place or you were not the head of a department, the Ministry of Public Building and Works required you to work in the same ambience as is found in a seaside boarding-house. You were spared only the cooking smells—and not always these.

The meeting which Martin remembered best was one attended by an expert on Bulgaria. He was a short, plump man with a thick accent, but his knowledge of that country was encyclopaedic and covered everything from the colour of the trams in Sofia to the best place to buy a plastic mackintosh in Plovdiv. Martin had inquired rather anxiously how much of all this detail he was expected to store away and remember, to which Peacock had replied airily that, if the occasion arose, he would probably recall what was necessary. He had then, when the Bulgarian expert had gone out of the room to fetch a further map, explained that the man was a first-rate fellow, but selectivity was not his strong point.

'He just can't help being a walking-talking guide-book cum Christmas catalogue,' Peacock had concluded, as the expert came bustling back into the room with a vast open map billowing before him.

It was at the final session that Martin said, 'Ought I not at least to know the names of the two girls who are going to be sitting next to me?'

'I was going to tell you those today,' Peacock said. 'The girl joining the bus at Munich is Anna Schmidt and the girl who takes her place is Paula Zwehl.' He watched Martin intently. 'All right?' he queried.

It struck Martin as a curious thing to ask, rather as if their names could be changed if he desired. He reckoned there were probably a million Anna Schmidts in Germany, though Zwehl was a less common name.

'Anna Schmidt and Paula Zwehl,' he murmured, as though this was required to commit their names to memory. 'And when I reach Istanbul, I just leave the bus and walk away?'

Peacock nodded. 'As easy as that. Your job'll be done.'

'Nobody's going to meet me there and debrief me, or anything of that sort?'

'If it's necessary to do that, we'll be able to find you. That applies all the way through. Don't call us, we'll call you is the order of the day. But if anything does go seriously wrong, you know what to do. But it won't, I'm sure of that. In fact your involvement in this whole operation would never have been approved if it had been felt there were serious risks attached.' He hunched his shoulders and lent forward over his desk. 'Whatever the public and press may sometimes choose to believe, we're a reasonably efficient lot and we certainly have a sense of responsibility. I like to think you wouldn't be helping us unless you were satisfied on those two scores.'

As he walked away from Peacock's office for the last time, Martin had pondered this, in particular his motive in agreeing to play what was admittedly no more than a walking-on part in this forthcoming piece of real life melodrama. It was true, he did accept that Peacock's organisation was efficient, extremely so in the care and thoroughness of their preparations, and also that its planners did have a sense of responsibility. But these attributes alone would not have lured him out of his comfortable rut. Nor was it a patriotic desire to serve his country which motivated him. No, it was something less estimable than that. It was the same motive which had taken him to Berlin a few years back. The appeal to masculine vanity and the challenge of breaking with routine after reaching an age when this became increasingly difficult.

'I live in a deep, satin-lined rut,' he was apt to say to friends, with a mixture of gratitude and resignation.

Well, here was a chance of clambering out of his rut, if only to prove to himself that he still had the ability to do so—the will-power to accept a challenge, a challenge which presented hidden risks.

Peacock had accompanied him to the entrance of the building and shaken hands at their final parting.

'Have a good trip and enjoy Istanbul,' he had said, as though seeing off a lucky customer on holiday.

CHAPTER THREE

They had shaken off the outskirts of Munich and were humming down the autobahn towards Salzburg before Martin cast so much as a covert glance at his companion.

She sat gazing out of the window behind her dark glasses, holding a cigarette close to her mouth and supporting that arm at the elbow with her other. She had small regular features and what Martin judged to be a naturally pale complexion. She wore dark lipstick which suited her better than any of the newer, lighter shades would have done. Her hair was dark brown and from time to time she would give her head a shake as though to resettle its fall. It was a gesture which reminded Martin of a horse's half-hearted efforts to drive flies away. He reckoned she was in her early thirties. So far she had not so much as given him a look.

The autobahn stretched straight ahead towards the mountains and the frontier with Austria. It was curious to recall that thirty years ago when the road had been built, its bold new conception of high-speed travel had excited admiration and envy all over the world. Now, in an age of ultra modern motorways, express-ways and free-ways, it seemed rather narrow and none too smoothly surfaced.

Martin decided it was time to take muster of some of his fellow passengers. As far as he could tell, he was the only English-speaking one on board. There was a group of about eight Persians, who, he gathered, had been working in Germany and were going home on holiday. They were enormously gregarious and voluble and gave the bus the air of a school outing. Mr Gursan appeared to have thrown in his lot with them and to be the centre of the explosions of laughter which from time to time drowned all other sounds.

Hans was driving and Ali, the co-driver, moved up and

down the bus adding his own contribution as life and soul of the party.

'Ah, my English friend,' he said, pausing beside Martin on one of his peregrinations to the ice-box at the back of the bus, 'you are fine, I hope.'

'Very fine,' Martin said with a smile.

'Where you live? In London?'

'Yes.'

'Very fine place, London. You like Soho?'

'I do indeed.'

'I have many fine times in Soho.' His grin broadened. 'But I not married then. No wife, no babies.' He diverted his gaze at Anna Schmidt. 'You also speak English, lady?'

She turned her head, eyes utterly masked by her spectacles, and said in an expressionless voice, 'Nein, ich spreche nur Deutsch.'

'The lady speaks only German,' Ali said to Martin. 'You sprechen the Deutsch?'

'Ein bisschen.'

'That is very fine. You will be able to speak together. Very important: Istanbul long way from here.' He departed with the happy countenance of a successful match-maker.

Since Anna Schmidt had returned her own attention to the view out of the window, Martin continued his survey of his fellow passengers.

Immediately in front of him sat a somewhat severe-looking, middle-aged woman, whose name he had caught as Fraülein Benzl. She had the almost caricatured appearance of a school-mistress and Martin conjectured that whatever her destination she was in search of culture.

In the two seats across the aisle from Fraülein Benzl sat a couple whose name he later found out to be Doctor and Frau Springer. Dr Springer was slight, had silvery hair and wore a pair of pince-nez which Martin thought to have gone out of fashion when he was a child. They were rimless and looked acutely uncomfortable, not to mention precarious. Frau Springer was many years her husband's junior. She was a handsome, rather than pretty, woman with blonde hair pulled back into a bun in the nape of her neck. Her face was angular, with the skin drawn tight over the cheekbones and she had about her an air of great composure.

At a guess, Martin would have said that she had once nursed her present husband and subsequently married him.

There was no one in either of the seats on the opposite side of the aisle from Martin and Anna Schmidt and no one in the row behind them, which was the back row of all.

Martin accepted it as part of Peacock's careful planning that they had no one at all sitting either behind them or at the same level.

The Austrian frontier came and went and Ali took over the wheel from Hans. The stewardess who had introduced herself as Toni made the occasional routine inspection of her passengers and fetched Coca-Cola for the thirsty from the ice-box at the back.

Martin inquired whether there was anything apart from Coke and was given, to his subsequent regret, a sticky orange-coloured drink which tasted of distilled swede.

In about the third hour he began to feel drowsy, lulled by the motion of the bus, its warmth and the utter normality of their progress. On present showing he reckoned that Anna Schmidt could be replaced by a Nile washer-woman without his fellow passengers so much as noticing. They all seemed completely uninterested in the couple at the back.

As he drifted off into forty winks, he wondered what Anna Schmidt was thinking about at that moment and whether she had been told as little about him as he had been told about her. So far they had exchanged not a word, but surely she must be wondering about him, too . . .

In the reflection of the bus window, Anna Schmidt noticed that Martin had nodded off and decided that this was her opportunity to study him unobserved.

She had already come to the conclusion that he had been well chosen for the part and she had been impressed by his relaxed air. She did not know what he did, and she had not even been told his name, but he looked to her like the manager of a large bank or perhaps the chairman of a prosperous family business. It had not occurred to her that he might be a lawyer since he in no way resembled any of that profession she had ever met. To her, lawyers were functionaries like minor civil servants.

As she looked at him now, she decided that she liked his appearance. He was thoroughly masculine and had a generally friendly air about him. In different circumstances she would rather have enjoyed getting to know him. But that was ruled out, other than . . . other than nothing! Brian Hart's instructions had been as explicit on the point as had Peacock's to Martin.

Anna Schmidt had never heard of Peacock, any more than Martin had heard of Hart, though the two men were well acquainted with one another and were members of the same organisation.

She supposed that Martin's briefing had been on the same lines as her own, though, as a professional, she was aware that this was not necessarily so. The need-to-know principle was sometimes used as an excuse for telling only half-truths and sometimes for insinuating untruths.

But in the present instance she felt sure that their briefings must coincide. There was no sense in it otherwise.

'This is a rescue operation, Anna,' Brian Hart had told her. (Anna was, in fact, her true name, though not Schmidt.) 'We want to get out a girl called Paula Zwehl. She's in East Germany at the moment, but she's going to be in Bulgaria shortly as secretary to a delegation of scientists and that's where we plan to lift her out. If you're wondering why you've been selected for a part in this, the reason is that you and Paula Zwehl bear a certain physical resemblance. Anyone knowing you both wouldn't be likely to confuse which was which, but it's one of those superficial resemblances and it's sufficient for our purpose.'

'What exactly am I supposed to do?' she had asked. 'And who exactly is Paula Zwehl?'

'You don't need to know anything more about Paula Zwehl than I've already told you,' Hart had said, giving her a friendly pat on the knee. 'As to what you're supposed to do, that I'm about to tell you. Paula Zwehl is going to be under fairly close observation all the time she's abroad—not just she, but the whole delegation for that matter—and so we have had to plan accordingly. The basis of the plan is the conjurer's sleight of hand.'

She had looked mystified as he had intended she should and he had gone on, 'While the attention of the audience is focused on your innocent right hand, you bring off the trick with your left. Got it?'

'Please, Brian,' she had said in a worried tone. 'Tell me what I have to do and don't play your guessing games.'

They were speaking in German, since Anna knew no more than a couple of dozen English words and Hart was completely bilingual.

21

He had smiled at her in a manner which always made her slightly uneasy. The smile suffused his face and his eyes twinkled, but she had the impression that his thoughts were all the time whirring away like lethal machinery.

'A decoy plan,' he had continued. 'That's what we've devised. A decoy plan and you're the decoy!'

'I am still waiting for you to explain the plan to me,' she had said a trifle irritably after he had sat back and observed her reaction for several seconds.

'Paula Zwehl is got out quite a different way, but you don't need to know the details of that; you see, you have nothing at all to do with the genuine escape plan. But nothing! The point is, however, that we let them think that she's going to be smuggled out of Bulgaria on this bus you'll be travelling on. At a given point—we'll come to that later—you wrap your head in a scarf, play around with your make-up and generally alter your appearance a bit so that our friends on the other side think that an exchange has taken place, and that you are, in fact, Paula Zwehl. Meanwhile Paula Zwehl will be quietly got out some other way. Now, do you see what I meant by conjurer's sleight of hand?'

'I do see,' she had said thoughtfully.

'And there'll be this Englishman in the seat beside you, who will swear, if necessary, that you're still the same person who has been on the bus since Munich—which, of course, you will be.'

'How far should I try and alter my appearance?' she had asked at a subsequent meeting.

'We'll give you something which'll bring on a streaming dose of hay fever. Something which'll make you look puff-eyed and runny-nosed and make your sinuses go berserk. In those circumstances, it would be quite natural for you to wrap your head up in a scarf. Anything to hide your blotchy face,' he had added with a laugh.

And now she was on the bus, with the real moment of truth not very many hours ahead.

She wondered what her seat companion felt about his part in this decoy operation. It was too bad for someone that things were not going to work out as planned—the more so as he looked an agreeable person. But that was not her responsibility and personal feelings were of no relevance, she told herself.

She lit another cigarette and returned her gaze out of the window.

CHAPTER FOUR

Night had fallen by the time they crossed from Austria into Yugoslavia and there was still a three-hour drive ahead to Zagreb, where they were due to stop the night.

As darkness closed in, so silence fell among the passengers, rather as though they were a cage of noisy parrots who had been covered up for the night. There was little other traffic about and they made good time save when the road abruptly became a rutted cart-track which it unaccountably did every so often. Hans was driving and Martin was filled with admiration for the sheer professional skill with which he handled the bus. Ali, for once, was sitting quietly in the co-driver's seat, smoking a cigarette and exchanging the occasional word with Toni, the stewardess.

It was a dark night without even a star to be seen and Martin had given up trying to observe what sort of countryside they were passing through. From time to time they came to a village and the road was suddenly, incongruously illuminated by harsh sodium lights which disclosed an appearance of poverty. There were few people to be seen save in what Martin assumed to be the equivalent of the village pub, a sparsely furnished room of a few chairs and tables, badly lit by a naked bulb and with men seated with glasses before them.

They usually passed through these villages like an express train and were out into the black countryside again with only a blurred impression as a memory.

Not only was Hans a superb driver, but it seemed he must know every inch of the way between Munich and Istanbul.

Martin glanced at Anna Schmidt who was sitting very quietly. She was still wearing her opaque glasses and it was impossible to tell whether she was awake or asleep. From the way she held her head, he inferred that she must be awake.

He himself was feeling wide awake and now that there was nothing to see outside, his mind was consumed with boredom. Also it seemed that he had spent a lifetime on the bus: he did not even remember such a long drawn-out day. Indeed, he had been on the bus over twelve hours and still he and the girl had not exchanged a word. It was the most astonishing set-up once you stopped to consider it. A man and a woman trundling across south-east Europe next to each other in a bus, their fates tenuously linked in some kind of way which neither was fully aware of, and yet not on permitted speaking terms.

For his part, the more he thought about it, the more he was curious to know what was going to happen to Anna Schmidt after the exchange had taken place.

'You don't need to worry about her,' Peacock had said. 'That's all taken care of and it's not a part of the operation which affects you.'

He was not exactly worried about her—well, certainly not yet, but he was damned curious to know how she, in her turn, was rescued and what was going to befall her in Bulgaria after she had left the bus. He could only hope, for her sake, that Peacock was as omnipotent as he appeared to be, since the thought of her just being abandoned to her fate was highly disquieting.

While Martin was brooding on the situation, she moved in her seat and he seized his opportunity of speaking to her.

'I shall be glad when we reach Zagreb. I've had enough of this bus for one day,' he said in his fluent, if imprecise, German.

She half-turned her head towards him. 'Yes, it is a long way. And tomorrow we leave at seven o'clock, so we can't lie in bed.'

Her voice was pleasant, though Martin thought he detected a note of nervousness in it. Well, that was understandable! But she was obviously a pretty brave girl or she would not be in this racket.

Before he could say anything further, she went on in a slightly louder tone, which could have been overheard by the people in the nearby seats if they happened to be tuned in, 'You speak good German. I heard you tell the driver you were English, but you must have spent some time in Germany?'

'Yes, I was a student at Munich University a good many years ago. I learnt to speak it then.'

She nodded. 'You are going to Istanbul?'

'Yes. I've been promising myself a visit there for a long time. It's certainly one of the cities of the world to capture one's imagination. The Seraglio, the Blue Mosque, the Golden Horn.'

'Yes, it is very beautiful.'

'You know it?'

'My brother teaches art at a school there.'

Martin made an interested noise and wondered if she really

did have a brother who taught art there. He saw now that there was something slightly unreal in carrying on a conversation with her. Rather like a TV panel game where the contestants have to guess when they are being told the truth and when confronted by whopping lies.

At any rate, they had now made contact, which was the natural thing for them to have done, even if their dialogue bore little relation to events. Not even Peacock could have taken exception to it!

About half an hour later, they began to enter Zagreb and shortly afterwards pulled up outside a drab-looking hotel in an equally drab-looking street.

'It is half past ten and dinner will be served immediately,' Toni, the stewardess, announced. 'Tomorrow morning we get up at six o'clock, so come quickly now please.'

Martin stood in the aisle and stretched. He felt far stiffer than he normally did after three strenuous sets of tennis singles. He stood back to let Anna Schmidt go ahead of him and she gave him a small, weary smile.

'I am glad we have arrived,' she said. 'I am very tired. I shall not wait for dinner.'

'Nor I,' Martin echoed. 'It's bed straight away for me.'

By the time he reached the lobby, Tony was distributing room keys to a clamouring throng. She looked flustered and it soon became apparent that a number of people who wanted single rooms were not going to get them. A stolid faced night porter was standing on the other side of the reception counter saying every time she appealed to him, 'All nice double rooms. For one night, they share.' He would then point arbitrarily at two of the same sex and say, 'You, you, share, yes?'

'No,' Martin said firmly on being paired off with Dr Springer. He hoped he was reflecting Frau Springer's wishes as well, she having momentarily disappeared. Dr Springer himself seemed unaware of what was happening. He just stood looking bewildered while people jostled around him.

By standing at the end of the queue and by refusing to budge until he was assured of a single room, Martin had the satisfaction of witnessing the night porter's capitulation and of finally being shown to one—or rather of finding his way to the room whose key number he bore.

It was on the fourth floor and he flung his suitcase on to the bed and flopped down gratefully beside it. He felt utterly whacked and realised that despite the outward normality of the day he had almost exhausted his resources of nervous energy. And the sombre thought was that tomorrow would be worse. Tomorrow they would be entering Bulgaria and he might be called upon to enact the small deception he had been brought all this way for. Small! The nearer he came to performing it, the less plausible and the more transparently foolish it seemed. All he had was Peacock's word that it would not prove to be so, but he had been discovering that Peacock's word diminished in persuasiveness the farther he got from London.

He opened his suitcase and pulled out his pyjamas and washing things. There was a basin over in one corner of the room with a steadily dripping tap and he went across to clean his teeth. An evil smell was coming from the waste-pipe and after he had finished washing, he put the plug back in to try and bottle it up.

The bed was reasonably comfortable and he lay back with a sigh of relief that the day was at an end, even though it had brought tomorrow nearer. Happily he had never had difficulty in getting to sleep and this was so whatever the weight of the problems on his mind.

He had no idea how long he had been asleep, nor yet what had awakened him save that it was some untoward noise. With heart beating faster, he half-propped himself up on one elbow and listened intently.

At first, his ears rang only with silence, then he heard the handle of his door being softly turned and could see from the corridor light which seeped beneath the door that someone was standing outside.

He sprang out of bed and switched on the light all in one movement. Without bothering to put on his dressing-gown, he ran to the door, unlocked it and pulled it open. The corridor with its path of worn coconut matting running down the centre was empty, and Martin hesitated a second before tiptoeing four doors along to where it made a right angle turn. As he looked down, a door opened and Mr Gursan stuck his head out. He raised a mild eyebrow at Martin's appearance and then stepped into the corridor. He was fully dressed.

'You don't have the dinner?' he inquired genially.

'No, I went straight to bed. What time is it?'

'Midnight. It was a good dinner. Now we all sleep well.'

He went back into his room with a cheery wave of the hand and Martin, feeling both non-plussed and uneasy, returned to

26

his. Non-plussed at being seen scouting round the corridors in his pyjamas like an actor out of a bedroom farce: uneasy because someone had been trying his bedroom door and he had no idea who it was. Furthermore, what had brought Mr Gursan to his door?

As he got back into bed, he tried to remember who had the rooms either side of his. He was almost sure that one was Fräulein Benzl, and the other was one of the bus crew. Yes, he remembered now: Hans and Ali were sharing the room on the side of his nearest the bend in the corridor. But he felt almost certain that he would have heard their door open and close if it had been one of them. The thing he now recalled about the incident was that one second the handle was being tried by someone immediately outside the door, the next they had disappeared and there had been no sound whatsoever either of human movement or of doors being opened and shut. It could only mean one thing, namely that his visitor was well practised in nocturnal stealth.

He got back into bed but it was an hour before sleep came to him again. After that, however, he knew nothing more until he awoke just before six o'clock. He felt refreshed, and then surprised as this fact registered itself on his mind. Though he invariably did sleep well, he was always slow to come to life in the morning and had become used to regarding the first half-hour of each working day as a period of the most sombre proportions. When the apocalypse struck, he knew for sure that it would be within that first half-hour.

Getting out of bed, he went across to the window and looked out. Uninspiring, non-conforming rooftops stretched away beneath his gaze. In the distance two tall, lifeless factory chimneys stood out against the horizon. So far, Zagreb had revealed nothing to commend itself to him. It was flat and grey and as uninteresting as a sheet of cast-iron.

He walked over to the wash basin and gingerly removed the plug, half-expecting to be driven back by the awful smell. It was still present, but seemingly less potent than it had been the previous evening.

By the time he had washed, shaved and dressed, and stuffed his things back into his case he was ready for breakfast, though not particularly confident about what he was likely to be offered, having regard to the earliness of the hour and the generally faded atmosphere of the hotel.

The group of Persians were already in the dining-room,

which was filled with the sound of their bright chirruping. They greeted him with cheerful smiles and a series of 'guten Morgens', as he went across and sat down next to Fräulein Benzl who was reading a guide-book which she held in the palms of her uplifted hands as though she was about to give utterance to selected passages. She glanced up as Martin took his seat and acknowledged his presence with a small nod, before resuming her reading.

Martin looked about him. There was a basket containing hunks of what turned out to be extremely dry bread, a small saucer of jam and another containing whorls of butter. He helped himself and then waited for the arrival of the unshaven, gummy-eyed youth in a crumpled white jacket who was going the rounds pouring out coffee.

When he reached him, Martin drank down the first cup before the youth had time to move away and indicated he wanted another. The youth refilled the cup and then stood there yawning as though to go on repeating the performance until the pot was empty.

'Genug,' Martin said firmly, pointing at his cup, and the youth drifted away. Because he was travelling on a German bus with mostly German passengers, it seemed proper that he should speak in German, though why he should do so to a Yugoslav waiter showed an absence of logic which struck him only afterwards.

He had almost finished his breakfast when Dr and Frau Springer came into the dining-room. Frau Springer was dressed in a completely different outfit from the previous day, the more noticeable since everyone else had merely clambered back into their original clothes. She was wearing a light beige dress of some silky material and had a pale blue cardigan draped over her shoulders. She guided her husband to an empty table in a distant corner of the room, which was not laid for breakfast, and declined to be dislodged by the elderly waiter who came bustling forward like a spider, the perimeter of whose web is under assault. Martin noticed that she buttered her husband's bread for him and cut it into manageable pieces while he watched her impassively. There was another ripple of mild disturbance when she rejected coffee for them both and demanded tea.

With nothing else to do, Martin gave them his covert attention, fascinated, in part, by the way Dr Springer's pince-nez wobbled on his nose as he chewed, but puzzled more than ever by their out-of-placeness on the bus. Most of the passengers were clearly on it because it was the cheapest way of getting to Istanbul and beyond. Those who were not using the service for this reason must, so far as Martin was concerned, be regarded with suspicion. And unrelievable suspicion, too, since Peacock's instructions excluded the possibility of trying to find out anything about them. But one thing was certain and that was that the Springers were not travelling by bus for reasons of economy. A chauffeur-driven Mercedes was more their line, Martin reckoned.

Finding that Fräulein Benzl was also watching them, Martin almost succumbed to the temptation of seeing whether she knew anything about them. He might indeed have succumbed, had she not at that moment briskly gathered up her guide-book and handbag and departed from the dining-room.

With only ten minutes to go, there was still no sign of Anna Schmidt and Martin experienced a faint tingle of anxiety lest something had already happened. The exchange had already taken place ... the original plan had been hastily abandoned for some sinister reason ... Was that why someone had tried to get into his bedroom last night?

Peacock had talked glibly about the need-to-know principle. But more and more did it occur to Martin that he knew damn all. He had embarked on this crazy journey, putting all his childlike trust in Nurse Peacock, but he would have done better to have examined the casting and made sure that Nurse Peacock was not really Bette Davis playing one of her demonic rôles. However, he was now committed and could only continue the grisly game and hope for the best.

After these and similar searing thoughts directed against Peacock and his brethren, it was something of an anti-climax to find Anna Schmidt sitting composedly in her seat in the bus staring out of the window through her enormous, dark spectacles. Martin almost wondered if she had slept in them.

'I didn't see you in the dining-room,' he remarked, after they had exchanged 'good mornings'.

'It is too early to eat breakfast. I just have a small cup of coffee in my room.'

'I'm glad to know that the hotel could manage that.'

'I made it myself.'

'Ah!'

Hans had taken his place at the wheel, Toni had counted them twice to make sure no one was missing and Ali was talking to half a dozen people at once, moving up and down the bus rather like a monkey swinging from branch to branch.

'You have very fine sleep?' he inquired of Martin.

'Very fine, thanks.'

'Good. Today is a long journey. Eight hundred kilometres, perhaps. But we have fine lunch in Belgrade and so we are strong again in afternoon.'

He swung off down the aisle to fraternise with some of his own compatriots and Martin turned to find that Anna Schmidt's attention had once more reverted to the window. He noticed that the hand which held her cigarette was trembling slightly and was sure that it had not done so yesterday.

Ignoring the signs that she did not wish to converse, he said abruptly, 'What time do we reach the Yugoslav–Bulgarian frontier? Do you happen to know?'

He thought at first that she was not going to answer; then, half-turning her head but without looking at him, she said, 'Not until after dark this evening, I think. Sofia is only one hour from the frontier and the timetable says we are due in Sofia at half past nine.'

Her tone had been mechanical, as if convention, and only convention, had required her to answer. And as soon as she finished speaking, she lay back with head rested to one side and, Martin assumed, eyes closed. Her meaning was as clear as if she had hung a 'Do Not Disturb' sign round her neck.

Later her head lolled farther over and she clearly had fallen asleep. She looked small and defenceless and frightened—yes, frightened even in sleep. What a revolting world it was, Martin reflected, that allowed girls such as Anna Schmidt to be used in this way! It was not that he was over-chivalrous or had Victorian ideas on a woman's place: it was just that an ordinary decent society should not employ girls on its dirtier assignments. He realised he was viewing the matter emotionally, and he could even hear Peacock's faint drawl saying, 'But my dear fellow, how do you imagine we can keep our society decent without the constant battle of wits with those who are trying to subvert our way of life?'

Well, everyone was two people, the rational and the emotional, and at the moment Martin's emotional self was calling the tune.

The road between Zagreb and Belgrade was remorselessly straight and ran across a flat cultivated plain for over two hundred seemingly endless miles.

They stopped once for half an hour at a new motel and Martin noticed that Anna Schmidt made straight for the ladies' room and did not emerge until the bus was about to depart. Whether this was done simply to avoid him, he did not know.

At lunch in Belgrade, she came into the hotel dining-room well after everyone else was served and joined the table of a mother and daughter of, Martin had gathered, Armenian descent who were travelling to Beirut. The daughter was a fat girl of about fourteen who went into prolonged gales of laughter every time anyone spoke to her. Martin had decided sourly quite early on that she was the more than perfect audience for the bus's self-appointed humorists. Immediately they regained the bus after lunch, Anna Schmidt turned her back towards him and ostentatiously composed herself for a siesta.

For a while Martin gazed out at the pleasantly undulating landscape which was in agreeable contrast to the morning's ride. It was a warm sunny afternoon and the countryside looked particularly peaceful in its varying shades of light green. Moreover, it was a good road and the tyres of the bus hummed their satisfaction as they sped along its surface, with Ali at the wheel. It was soon apparent that Anna Schmidt was not alone in seeking a siesta, as an infectious drowsiness claimed first one passenger then another.

Martin, however, determined to stay awake. The journey was half-completed and whatever was going to happen would be within the next twenty-four hours. He had studied the timetable and seen that they crossed into Bulgaria at half past eight this evening and out of that country into Turkey at five o'clock tomorrow afternoon. Some time during those twenty-one and a half hours, Anna Schmidt was due to be replaced at his side by another woman in such a way, if Peacock was to be believed, that no one was likely to notice that a swap had taken place...

The screaming implausibility of this seemed to grow with every mile they travelled, as did the temptation to compel Anna Schmidt to compare notes with him. What did she know that he didn't? And what right had Peacock to expect them not to converse about the matter which filled both their minds and upon which their futures hung.

With an effort, Martin suppressed his self-engendered indignation. It was a sign of his edginess and he would do well to

31

bring his adrenal glands under greater control. The one quality he was going to need to exhibit was cool judgment.

He forced his mind into more practical channels and tried to recall whether he had subconsciously noticed any little mark of suspicion among his fellow passengers. Whether he had seen any of them behaving out of pattern: any of them in unlikely earnest conversation.

Gazing at the backs of the heads in front of him in a mental roll call, he was unable, however, to think of one single movement which had appeared remotely suspicious.

Well, perhaps he and Anna Schmidt *were* the only two on the bus who were not all they seemed. Perhaps all the others *were* bona fide travellers whose only interest was in reaching their destination.

Certainly Peacock had said nothing to suggest that every other passenger would be an agent in somebody or other's pay. He had enjoined circumspection, but then he probably did that when his wife went shopping. It was second nature to him. On the other hand, Martin had somehow assumed that there were likely to be others on the bus who were also involved in Peacock's elaborate scheme: others who were interested in Anna Schmidt and her mysterious double.

He felt he could rule out the ebullient Persians. But what about the curious Dr and Frau Springer who seemed such misfits on a bus ride across the Balkans? And what to make of Fräulein Benzl who looked capable enough of running an intelligence network on her own? Or of Mr Gursan who seemed a cut above his compatriots on the bus and who, Martin had noticed, kept a keen eye on all about him, even if at this particular moment his head was sunk on his chest in sleep?

Martin realised that speculation was getting him nowhere. He had to maintain his trust in Peacock or ... Or nothing! There was no palatable alternative.

In the late afternoon they entered the town of Niš, where the Athens and Istanbul roads parted company. Soon afterwards they drove through a splendid gorge and then wound their way through wild hills on a road which deteriorated as the scenery became more spectacular.

Dusk was falling when they reached the frontier town of Dmitrovgrad. It seemed to Martin that the Yugoslav officials there showed an almost irresponsible haste and unconcern ushering them out of that country and on their way to the Bulgarian post a quarter of a mile farther along the road.

'Please all stay in your seats for passport control,' Toni announced. 'After that you may get out until we are ready to leave.'

A stern-faced young guard in uniform entered the bus, saluted them with polite formality and began to check their passports. He was a good-looking, country boy who gave Martin the impression of having been recently promoted to this important duty. He examined each passport with the gravity of someone searching for murder clues, meticulously comparing the owner with his photograph and turning the pages with a measure of deliberation so as to give even the innocent a sensation of unease.

Martin glanced at the passport which Anna Schmidt was holding ready in her lap. It was a West German one and was open at the page bearing a Bulgarian visa. Martin had a similar visa in his, which he had obtained before leaving London, on Peacock's instructions.

The guard was now examining the Springers' passports and frowning. He murmured something to them and Frau Springer replied, which caused him to frown more deeply. He unbuttoned his breast pocket and took out a notebook in which he slowly wrote for several seconds, while Dr Springer stared vaguely ahead of him and Frau Springer gazed fixedly out of the window. When he had finished writing, he moved impassively on, leaving Martin wondering what significance to place on this tiny ripple in the slow but otherwise perfectly smooth routine.

His attention was momentarily distracted by Ali, yawning prodigiously and obviously bored by the absence of activity. Hans was leaning against the steering-wheel watching events inside the bus through half-closed eyes.

The young guard arrived at where Martin and Anna Schmidt were sitting. The girl handed him her passport with the nonchalant air of a professional traveller and took no notice at all as he leafed his way slowly through it, before adding it to the pile beneath his arm. Martin then proffered his and watched him with a thumping heart as he examined it. Was it his imagination or did the guard really give it less cursory attention than he had the others?

He was still pondering this disconcerting thought when Toni announced that they could now leave the bus and that it would probably be half an hour or more before they were ready to depart.

The atmosphere was of a class of children released for the mid-morning break, as everyone got up and shook and stretched. There was a café which formed part of the frontier buildings and they drifted across to it.

Martin saw the young guard enter a lighted room alongside the café and put all their passports on a desk, behind which sat a much older man in uniform. Also in the room was a civilian in a leather coat and a wide-brimmed light grey felt hat, who seemed to Martin to bear all the stigmata of the security police.

The café was new and bright with a majestic espresso machine in the charge of a dark, flashing-eyed female who was already engaged in a bantering exchange with Ali. They talked in Turkish, though it was soon apparent that the woman could speak passable German. She had a deep, throaty voice and the sort of animal attraction which probably ensured that her bed was a place of constant activity.

He ordered a coffee, bought two picture postcards and moved to one end of the counter to observe the scene further. There was no sign of Anna Schmidt, nor of the Springers. Fräulein Benzl was turning the rack of postcards with a concentrated air while Mr Gursan watched her with a faintly puzzled expression.

Martin mentally shook himself. He really must guard against seeing significance where there was none. He felt like someone walking down a long corridor with a series of one-way doors which close with soft menace behind him. In the present instance he had just passed through the final one to find himself standing in a featureless room in cavernous darkness. That was how Bulgaria appeared to him at this moment.

To try and restore his sense of perspective, he gazed at the bright posters round the walls. They showed a Bulgaria of sunshine and blue sea, of enchanting lakes and benign mountains, and always a laughing, happy people. These were the posters of the State tourist office. There were others, however, which depicted square-jawed young men linking arms with merry, but determined-looking, young women, as together they gazed steadfastly into the future. In one, a large sheaf of golden wheat appeared to be sharing their hopes for the future: in another, the couple were joined by a huge tractor which managed to convey an impression of political consciousness.

'This is your first trip to Bulgaria, sir?'

Martin turned sharply to find a rather flabby man of about thirty staring at him with polite curiosity. It was the man he had noticed at the small tourist office counter over in one corner of the café. His accent was American—Brooklyn American.

'Yes, it is,' he replied slowly.

'Come over to the desk and I give you some pamphlets and maps. All free,' he added with a smirk. 'Balkantourist wants all visitors to Bulgaria to feel welcome.'

Martin followed him across the room.

'Now, here is a map of our country and this one here tells you all about our lovely Black Sea beaches and here is a list of hotels and ...'

'Before you go on,' Martin broke in, 'I ought to tell you that I'm off the bus. We're stopping tonight in Sofia and tomorrow we drive on to Istanbul.'

For a moment, the man looked downcast, then with a shrug he said, 'Never mind, keep them. I think you will find them interesting, particularly that one'—he tapped the Black Sea resort one—'perhaps it will inspire you to visit there on your way home. It really is very beautiful.' He grinned. 'As beautiful as California.'

'It's obvious that you've spent some time in America?' Martin said.

'Four years in our office in New York.'

'Did you enjoy that?'

'Oh yes. But I prefer my own country.'

'Incidentally, how did you know I was English?' Martin asked.

'You look like an Englishman,' the man replied, smiling again. 'And that, of course, is a compliment!'

Martin cocked a wry eyebrow at him, but said nothing. He was trying to decide what it was about him that he found repellent. The moist mouth and the discoloured teeth? The determined eagerness? The generally mongrel appearance? Perhaps all of them together making someone who excited instant, though indefinable, mistrust. Yes, that was it, he was the seedy con man.

Martin was relieved when Fräulein Benzl came across and enabled him to escape with his handful of pamphlets.

He stepped outside and bumped into Mr Gursan who was just coming back in.

'We go soon, you think?' Mr Gursan asked.

'I've no idea, but I hope so.'

'I hope, too.' There was a pause. 'You are from England, yes?'

'Yes. From London.'

'You are only Englishman on bus, yes?' Mr Gursan said with a chuckle.

'I gather so.'

'You go to Istanbul?'

'Yes.'

'You stay there long?'

'About a week, I hope.'

'You will like. Very beautiful place. Where you stay?'

Martin wondered how Peacock would have reacted to such blatant curiosity. However, unlike the Balkantourist official, Mr Gursan managed to inspire his trust. Nevertheless, he did not intend, so to speak, to place his life in the Turk's hands.

'I'm not sure,' he answered.

'The Hilton Hotel is very fine. Good vista of the Bosphor. You are on holiday?' he added keenly.

'Yes.'

'Of course! No one travel by bus on business.' He let out another cheerful laugh. Then with a shrug which seemed to sum up the state of the whole stupid world, he gave Martin a broad wink and strolled back inside the café.

Martin walked beyond the range of reflected light coming from the building and stood gazing into the darkness. The air was warm, but with a scented freshness about it and everything seemed very peaceful. Half-way up a slope on the far side of the frontier post stood what appeared to be a new motel. A naked bulb hung in one room where he could see a man decorating a wall. But apart from that and a porch light, the place was in darkness. Looking back down the road, he could see the Yugoslav Customs building and the striped pole across the road beside it. It seemed a decade since they had passed through there. In fact, a glance at his watch showed that it was exactly forty-five minutes ago.

As he strolled back towards the building, he noticed that a blind had been drawn over the window of the room into which their passports had been taken. When he reached the window, he took a quick sideways look through the crack between the edge of the blind and the window-frame.

Sitting at ease on a chair against one wall was Frau Springer. As he watched her, she threw back her head in a spontaneous laugh. He was so surprised by the scene that he just stood staring in for what seemed an eternity. Then recalling the possible danger of attracting attention to himself he moved quickly away from the window and out once more beyond the range of light.

Hans and Ali and Toni now came out of the Customs office and Ali ran across to the bus and sounded the horn vigorously.

At last they were off! Martin heard footsteps in the darkness behind him and turned to see Anna Schmidt a couple of yards from him. She did not appear to notice him as she made her way back to the bus.

Now where had she been all this time? She had come from the direction of the unfinished motel. Or had she simply been standing in the darkness, rather as he had, only a bit farther away?

With waves from the women in the café and one or two others, they pulled away on the final short leg of the day's run to Sofia.

It was not until they had arrived there and Martin was unpacking in the hotel bedroom that it occurred to him to glance at the pamphlets he had been given at the frontier. He had thrown them down on the bed and now picked up the one extolling Bulgaria's Black Sea resorts. The one the shifty-looking tourist official had especially commended to his attention.

With casual interest, he opened it out.

Written in schoolboy script across one corner was:

'Don't catch Anna's bad cold.'

CHAPTER FIVE

For a full minute, Martin just stared at the message, hoping for some sudden flash of comprehension. But none came. Then he scanned both sides of the unfolded pamphlet to discover whether there was anything further written on it. He even held it up to the light to see if there were any impressions of further writing, since the original message had been written with a ball-point pen. But there was nothing.

He laid the open pamphlet on his bed and stood staring down at it, hands in pockets and shoulders hunched forward the way he sometimes studied a brief in Chambers.

He read the printed matter in the vicinity of the message in the hope that this might somehow throw light on its meaning. But it did not. The message stood unrelated to anything else in the pamphlet and could just as well have been conveyed on any other bit of paper. Any bit of paper, that is, which the tourist official could have passed to Martin without arousing suspicion.

The only thing he could do was to pummel his brain until it made some sense of the message.

To start with, Anna was clearly Anna Schmidt, but so far as he had observed she had shown no signs of having a cold. Not that it seemed likely that the author of the message was concerned with the transfer of a few germs. No, the message was clearly a warning; but a warning of what? Events planned in London weeks ago were going to fructify within the coming few hours. Was this a reminder of the need to dissociate himself completely from Anna Schmidt in whatever was about to befall them? It could be that. It made sense. Moreover, it meant that the unlikeable tourist official must be one of Peacock's far-flung servants.

If he was not that, then he must of necessity be in someone else's security service and the implications of that were more than alarming...

Martin straightened up and walked over to the window, where he stood looking down at a broad square. Five or six roads fed it with traffic and tram lines intersected in the centre. At one end of the square was a mosque with a minaret, with another church of Eastern appearance nearby. The building opposite was hung with red banners covered with slogans and with photographs of political leaders of the U.S.S.R. and of Bulgaria itself. The square was full of people waiting for trams or walking home.

It was a scene of utter normality in one sense. But to Martin at this moment it was one of claustrophobic fear. He felt utterly alone and surrounded by hidden faces of menace. And yet there was only one thing he could do, grit his teeth and go on. If only because to back out now was a practical impossibility.

'The odds are you'll have a trouble-free run,' Peacock had confidently predicted, and Martin Ainsworth, the seeker after mild adventure and a break with urban routine, had chosen to believe him.

Turning from the window, he gave himself a vicious mental kick and heaped a mound of choicer curses on Peacock's head. He refolded the pamphlet, stuck it in his pocket and went downstairs.

The lobby might at first glance have been that of any large western European hotel. It was only at second glance that one noticed the reception counter was staffed by middle-aged females in home-knitted cardigans and the head concierge was dressed in a left-over outfit of a municipal baths attendant.

Though the lobby was full, Martin did not see any of his own party. There was a group of men near the lifts speaking German and three Africans, two men and a girl, sitting over on a settee. Martin noticed that they were talking in English.

He handed his key to one of the middle-aged receptionists and said in German, 'I am just going out for a stroll.'

Afterwards, he tried to analyse his motive in telling her his movements—the more so as she had obviously neither understood what he said nor worried about the fact. It could only be something to do with a sense of guilt and with the determination to appear normal and beyond anyone's suspicion. Perhaps, it was as well she had not understood or such a gratuitous piece of information might have aroused her suspicions.

He walked down one side of the square and turned into a broad thoroughfare which was full of shops and cafés. Some way along he passed the floodlit mausoleum of Dimitrov guarded by two upright sentries in handsome uniform.

For half an hour, he walked at a steady pace along the tree-lined pavements, breathing in deeply the calm evening air and gradually regaining his composure, which had been badly dented by the sudden threat of unidentified danger implicit in the message.

At one point, he crossed a street and dropped the pamphlet, which he had already torn into small pieces, in a waste-paper basket at a tram halt. After that, he somehow felt better.

The hotel lobby looked the same as when he had left it, even to the three Africans still deep in conversation on the settee (probably putting the Marxist–Leninist world to greater rights, he reflected). He went across to collect his key.

'You are Mr Ainsworth?' the receptionist queried, addressing him in careful English. She was a different woman from the one to whom he had handed his key on going out.

'Yes.'

'There has been a mistake, Mr Ainsworth. You are now in

room 426. It is on the same floor, but it is a quieter room. Your things have already been taken to the new room.'

'I'd made no complaint about the noise in my other room,' he observed, with the rising resentment of an Englishman who feels he is being pushed around by officialdom.

'Pardon?'

'I preferred the other room,' he said firmly.

'This room is quieter.'

'How do you know I like quiet rooms?'

She shrugged. 'Here is key of 426. Sleep well.'

'Why the hell should I sleep well?' he ground out, infuriated by her stony refusal to explain the move.

'Excuse please. I have other business,' she remarked, and walked away, leaving him with the key to his new room.

He was just about to enter the lift when Toni came dashing up.

'Thank goodness, I've found you, Herr Ainsworth. There has been a change of plan tomorrow. We do not have breakfast here but at a place in the mountains, one hour's drive from Sofia. That means we must now leave at half past six.'

'What's the reason for the change?'

'I don't know. It is ordered by Balkantourist and we have to do as they say. It has happened before.'

'It has?'

'Oh, yes. Sometimes they re-route us because they want us to see some new hotel or resort which they have opened. It is good advertisement, but it makes us late arriving in Istanbul.'

'I follow. Incidentally, did you know that I've been moved to another bedroom?'

'Yes, they tell me.'

'What reason did they give?'

'They had promised your original room to a very old client of the hotel. He always has that room and you were given it in error.'

'I wonder!' Martin murmured as he bade her good night and went up in the lift.

As far as he could see, room 426 was no different from the first room, apart from facing the other way. The view from its window was dominated by a large building which was surmounted by a huge, glowing red star.

The obvious reason for moving him was because this room was bugged and the other was not. That either meant they were intending to compromise him themselves or believed it

40

possible that he might be receiving a visitor of his own.

Well, he would lock and bolt the door and not open it until he vacated the room in the morning. That would take care of that! But if the room was bugged, then the odds were that it was also under visual control. Perhaps they hoped to catch him reading some compromising document. He felt an upward tilt to his morale that he had had the foresight to dispose of the message-bearing pamphlet. Just supposing he had left it lying on his bed in the other room!

Now that the chips were down, or half-down, he felt that much better. Such is the curiously illogical working of the mind under emotional stress.

It was with an almost jaunty nonchalance that he undressed and got into bed. He hoped he had given the secret police a frustrated evening's viewing. With this morale-raising thought, he leant across and switched off the light.

The ringing of his bedside telephone at half past five the next morning quickly dispelled, however, the last remnants of the euphoria which had seen him to sleep. He washed and shaved with a sense of doom. This was D-Day! A D-Day whose long prepared battle plan might already have been overtaken by events! And he was in the first assault wave!

He felt slightly better when he was back in the familiar surroundings of the bus.

Ali and Hans were there looking tousled and unshaven. The chirruping Persians were for once subdued and several of them had already gone back to sleep. Dr Springer, on the other hand, looked as though he had just been laundered. He reminded Martin of an extinct old bird. His wife was wearing a cream-coloured head-scarf, which from behind gave her the appearance of a nurse. Fräulein Benzl was, as usual, composed and alert, with her guide-book open on her lap.

He glanced around. Everyone was present save Anna Schmidt. Of her, there was no sign at all.

He looked towards the hotel entrance and saw Toni coming out accompanied by a short, thick-set man with a blond crew-cut who was carrying a shiny, plastic document case. They came round behind the bus and got in, the newcomer taking the seat normally occupied by Toni. She exchanged a few whispered words with Hans who started the engine and was about to drive off, when Martin jumped to his feet.

'Hey! Someone's missing, we're not all here yet,' he called out. As everyone turned in his direction, he added, 'The lady in the seat next to me hasn't come yet.'

For a moment, nobody said anything, but Martin noticed that Toni glanced quickly at Hans, who had stood up and was facing down the bus towards him. It was Hans who spoke.

'She became ill during the night,' he said in a flat tone. 'She is not fit to travel and is staying in Sofia. There is nothing to worry about, the doctor says she will be all right in a few days.'

He turned abruptly round and sat down and a second later was easing the bus away from the kerb. It was almost as though the crew realised some distraction was called for, since Toni at once seized the microphone and began a series of announcements. One half of Martin's mind listened, while the other half tried to grapple with this quite unpredicted development. A development which vitiated, in one, the whole purpose of his being on the bus. Peacock's plan was no more, and Martin felt like the victim of one of his nightmares in which he would dream that he was appearing in the wrong court.

'Ladies and Gentlemen,' Toni was saying, 'I am very happy to introduce you to Mr Rogov of Balkantourist who will travel with us today and tell us about those parts of his country through which we shall be passing. Mr Rogov.'

She handed the microphone to the crew-cut man beside her who began addressing them in German.

'My name is Dmiter Rogov, ladies and gentlemen, and I welcome you to Bulgaria on behalf of Balkantourist. We are sure you will enjoy your stay in our beautiful country. We are now leaving Sofia behind us and in one hour we come to the beautiful mountain resort of Borovets where we will have our breakfast...' Martin switched off his attention as the guide rolled out a mass of statistics, covering the country's topography, distribution of population, main industries and cultural achievements.

It was a question from Fräulein Benzl which brought Martin's attention right back into focus again.

'I see from my map,' she said reprovingly, 'that Borovets is not on our scheduled route. Why are we making this detour?'

Their new guide appeared momentarily non-plussed. Then he said, 'It is because the main road between Sofia and Plovdiv is closed. A part of it is closed, that is, and so we go through Borovets. But I am sure you will be glad when you have seen the most beautiful countryside.'

'Why is the main road closed?' Fräulein Benzl asked, without allowing herself any time to be influenced by the prospective beauties of the countryside.

'For repairs,' the guide replied promptly—far too promptly, it seemed to Martin—before going on hurriedly, 'And now on our left we see the beautiful new marina where the people can swim and boat and disport themselves...' There followed a turgid account of the types of building materials used on the project and of the true Socialist enthusiasm shown by those engaged in its construction.

Meanwhile Martin, whose breakfast appetite had completely vanished, tried to take fresh stock of his situation. A countryside which would normally have held his attention passed by the window unnoticed. He was vaguely aware of a lake beside which they drove for several miles and of steep, wooded hills, but it might have been almost anywhere for the impact it made on his mind.

Anna Schmidt had gone and no one had taken her place. These two simple facts chased each other round his mind like two dogs tearing round a garden, and just as fruitlessly. He wondered whether Peacock was at this moment trying to get fresh instructions through to him—assuming he even knew what had happened. He must be more than ever observant of everything around him so as not to miss any attempt to communicate with him. And if he did not receive any fresh instructions, all he could do would be to sit tight and hope that in six or seven hours' time he would be safely across the border and in friendly Turkey. He tried to project his mind ahead to when he was home again and would make a good dining-out story of the whole affair; or as much of it as he could properly tell. In true English fashion, he would underplay his part and reveal himself at his most urbane.

Unhappily, these attempted injections of self-confidence were not notably successful since the more realistic side of his mind would not allow him to forget that he was in an extremely disagreeable situation on any reckoning of the score.

He was aware of Toni coming down the aisle on one of her visits of inspection of the clutter of equipment stacked on the rear seat of the bus.

As she drew level with him he said, 'I'm sorry about Fräulein Schmidt. What actually is wrong with her?'

'She has a very bad cold and the colic.' She smiled faintly. 'A bus ride is not very comfortable in those circumstances.'

'Indeed, no! Was she taken ill during the night?'

'Yes. The night porter got a doctor for her.'

'Did you see her before we left?'

She shook her head. 'She had been transferred to hospital.'

'To hospital! She must have been bad then!'

'Hotels do not like sick persons in their rooms. They cannot look after them properly. It is always necessary to go to hospital if you become sick in a hotel. Is not so in England?'

'Certainly, if you're badly sick.'

'Fräulein Schmidt was badly sick, but will be better in a few days. That was what the doctor told the manager. All arrangements have been made for her to resume her journey as soon as she is well enough.'

She stood with a faintly quizzical expression as though waiting to see whether he had anything further to ask. He was aware that he had defied Peacock's instructions in exhibiting such blatant curiosity, but circumstances alter cases and he was on his own now.

'Have you had passengers fall suddenly ill like this before?' he asked in a tone which he tried to keep casual.

A guarded look came over her face. 'Not since I have worked with the company. But I am sure you need not worry. They have very good doctors in Bulgaria.'

'I'm sure they have, too. I was merely thinking that it's not an experience I should welcome. Falling sick in a country where I didn't know the language, I mean.'

'She will be well looked after. Now, if you will excuse me...'

She continued to the back of the bus and a couple of minutes later returned to her place, passing Martin with an obvious determination not to get drawn into further conversation.

Shortly afterwards, Mr Gursan left his seat and strolled back to where Martin was sitting.

'Pretty scenery,' he said, nodding towards the window.

'Very,' Martin replied with a brief nod.

'So you have lost your pretty companion?' Mr Gursan went on, eyeing him intently.

'The stewardess tells me she was taken to hospital in the night.'

Mr Gursan cocked his head on one side and pursed his lips in an expression of reserved judgment.

'And what is wrong with her?'

'Colic, the stewardess said.'

'You know her long time?'

Martin assumed an expression of puzzled surprise. 'I don't know her at all. I'd never met her before getting on this bus.'

'You not travel together?'

'No, we certainly weren't. We just happen to have been allocated seats next to one another.'

'Nice for you to have pretty girl to talk to,' Mr Gursan observed with a roguish grin.

'Except that she didn't seem to want to talk very much.'

'Perhaps she was feeling sick all the way.'

'Very likely that's the explanation.'

Mr Gursan nodded slowly, as though Anna Schmidt's silence and illness were now satisfactorily explained.

While they had been talking, the bus had been climbing in low gear up a winding road with thick woods on both sides. They swung round a final hairpin bend and the road levelled out. A hunting lodge appeared in a clearing on the left and a country mansion complete with Gothic turrets came into sight as the road bent away to the right.

'We are now entering Borovets,' the guide announced. 'Before the people's republic many rich persons had holiday villas here. Now Borovets is for all peoples and the villas have been turned into rest-homes and sanatoria for the workers.'

The bus came to a halt in the centre of the town and the guide went on, 'Please to follow me and we have our breakfast. It is hotel over there.' He pointed in the direction of a low, rambling building on a slope about two hundred yards away.

Although it was only eight o'clock in the morning, the narrow streets were full of people strolling in apparent aimlessness. Martin sniffed the clean, wood-scented air as he stepped from the bus. Apart from the strollers, it might have been a Swiss village, but their stolid expressions and group-mindedness clearly proclaimed this as an organised corner of a so-called workers' paradise.

As he was approaching the entrance to the hotel, he noticed Hans talking to the Balkantourist guide. They were standing beside the door and indicating the way to the dining-room.

Martin was almost the last to pass through. He had just done so when Hans addressed him.

'Excuse me, Herr Ainsworth, Herr Rogov wishes to speak to you.'

The guide looked embarrassed, but gave a confirmatory nod.

'Please come with me.'

'Where to?'

'Please come.'

'Tell me what you want.'

'Come! You will see.' The tone had become both flustered and peremptory.

Martin halted at the head of a flight of stairs leading to a floor below, which Rogov had begun to descend.

'I'm not moving another step until you tell me what all this is about,' he announced firmly.

The guide looked angry and impotent at the same time, rather like a new teacher faced with a recalcitrant sixth-former.

'It is about the lady who was sitting next to you in the bus ...' he said desperately.

'What about her?'

'She is in trouble.'

'I thought she was ill.'

Rogov shrugged helplessly. 'Please come and everything will be explained.'

'Come, where to?'

'To a room down here. There they will explain all.'

'Who are "they"?'

'Officials.'

'Police, do you mean?'

'They only want to ask you questions.'

'What about?'

'About the lady who is ill.'

'You said just now that she was in trouble.'

The guide's face now glistened like a polished apple.

'Please come quickly or we hold up the bus. Also you must have your breakfast. We do not have much time.' He turned and trotted down the stairs almost daring Martin not to follow him.

Slowly Martin did so. He felt he had made his gesture and shown that he was not prepared to be ordered around without some attempt at justification. On the other hand, he really had very little choice in the matter, particularly seeing that he was posing as one of the bus's ordinary passengers. As such he would naturally comply with any reasonably directed request.

Rogov turned right at the bottom of the stairs and led the way along a broad flag-stoned corridor. At the end of this, they turned left into a much narrower one which had a solid looking metal door at the far end. He gave a sharp knock on the door and opened it without waiting for any answer. Then holding it open with his back—it appeared to have an automatic closing device—he gestured Martin with a jerk of his head to enter.

Martin's first impression was of a large empty room with a low ceiling and a lot of exposed girders. There were also a number of pillars supporting the ceiling. The only light was at the far end where a bare table and some chairs were set out.

As he was taking in the scene, a figure appeared from behind one of the farther pillars.

'Please come and sit down, Mr Ainsworth,' a man said in excellent English.

Martin advanced across the room towards the table. The man who had addressed him was wearing a neatly cut blue suit and resembled a trim young bank clerk.

'I am here to act as interpreter,' he went on. 'These gentlemen have some questions they wish to ask you.'

Martin now, for the first time, observed that there were two other men in the room. And, moreover, the face of one of them was familiar. It was the face of the man he had seen in the room at the frontier post the previous evening. The room in which he had later caught sight of Frau Springer as she threw back her head in improbable laughter. The other man, who was clearly the senior of the two, had a Khrushchev-like head and a complexion like the skin of a grapefruit. He was smoking a cigar in a short holder and his eyes which seemed unbothered by the upward-drifting smoke were small and darkly glittering.

He motioned Martin to sit down on the opposite side of the table to him and his companion. The interpreter sat at his other side. Martin glanced round to find that Rogov had melted away. His assignment was apparently completed.

Bald-head spoke in his native tongue and then nodded at the interpreter who said, 'You are Mr Martin Ainsworth, are you not?'

'I am.'

'And you are British?'

'I am.'

'Where do you live?'

'In London.'

'And what is your work?'

'I'm a lawyer. An advocate, to be precise.'

'That is a barrister?'

'Correct.'

'What do you come to Bulgaria for?'

'I'm travelling through to Istanbul.'

'Why do you go to Istanbul by bus?'

'Because I thought it would be an interesting way of getting there.'

'No other reason?'

'No; no other reason at all.' Martin tried to make it sound as if he was giving a reasonable question an ultra reasonable answer.

In the pause which followed, he said, 'May I ask the purpose of these questions? If I've done anything wrong since I entered your country, please tell me; otherwise you have me at an unfair advantage.'

Bald-head's expression remained impassive as this was interpreted to him, but his eyes stayed fastened on Martin as they had been since the interrogation started. The interpreter finished speaking and bald-head began again in the same even, but slightly rasping, tone.

'How long have you known Fräulein Schmidt?'

Martin stared back with a hardened expression.

'Kindly explain who you mean?' he said.

'Fräulein Schmidt, the woman who was next to you in the bus. How long have you known her?'

'I'd never set eyes on her before joining the bus at Munich. And I don't even claim to know her now.'

'Why did you pretend not to know who she was when her name was mentioned just now?'

'Because although I'd heard her answer to the name of Schmidt on the bus, it is an extremely common name and, as I've already explained, I don't know her and you might have been referring to some other Schmidt.'

'You lie!'

'Is that a statement or a question?'

'You are a British spy, is it not so?'

'That's a lie!'

'You and Fräulein Schmidt are both spies. We have proof, so you had better admit it.'

'It's not true and I admit no such thing.' Martin found to his pleasurable surprise that he had been sufficiently stung by the circumstances of the interrogation to be able to respond with a show of genuine indignation.

'We have proof.'

'What proof?'

At this point the two men exchanged whispers while the interpreter leant across to listen. Martin was improbably reminded of three appeal judges going into a judicial huddle and this familiar image so cheered him up that he must have unconsciously smiled. He noticed bald-head glaring at him. Then the rasping voice addressed him again, with the interpreter's English breaking in just before the sentence was completed.

'Is it not true that you were sent to Bulgaria by the British imperialist spy organisation to commit a criminal provocation against the Bulgarian people?'

'No, it is not true,' Martin replied firmly, one small detached portion of his mind fascinated by the clichéed jargon.

'Is it not true that you came to make contact with the traitor agent Paula Zwehl?'

If they had sprung her name on him at the outset, they might have had a more rewarding reaction. As it was, it had been clear from very early on that Peacock's plan had been blown apart and the assumption was that the other side had learned every detail of it. In these circumstances, Martin had been braced against surprise after the first few questions.

'I don't know who you're talking about,' he said evenly.

'You are pretending that you have never heard of Paula Zwehl?'

'There's no pretence. I haven't.'

'You realise that you are in a very dangerous situation?'

'All I know is that I have done nothing wrong and that I resent this interrogation. I agreed to come down here as I understood you wanted me to help you. I didn't know I was going to be questioned like a suspect and I'd like to know by what authority you are doing so.'

As the interpreter finished translating this into Bulgarian, bald-head stubbed out his cigar with a vicious jab. It seemed to Martin that he was uncertain what to do next and if this was right, then it must surely mean that he had nothing against him and was running out of ideas for prolonging the interview.

The other man turned and spoke to bald-head and for several seconds they conversed, each of them from time to time casting a quick glance across the table at Martin. He decided that they were trying to find out whether he had any understanding of the language. In fact, though he had been listening in the hope of catching a familiar-sounding word, perhaps even a name, he had heard nothing of which he could make any sense at all.

The man he had seen at the frontier post suddenly got up and went across to a door which Martin had only noticed after sitting down. He opened it and motioned with his head to someone out of sight. Martin heard footsteps and just had time to register that they were female when Anna Schmidt appeared in the doorway.

She looked pale and drawn and was still wearing the pair of heavy dark glasses, which Martin had never seen her without. She came straight across and sat down on a chair which the interpreter had drawn up to the table. Behind her was a hard-faced female who could only have been a wardress in anyone's country.

After sitting down, Anna Schmidt stared at the surface of the table three feet in front of her. At no time did she give Martin so much as a glance.

Looking in her direction bald-head rasped out something and the interpreter took up his cue.

'You know this man?' he asked in German, indicating Martin.

'He sat next to me on the bus.'

'How long have you known him?'

'I had not met him before.'

'But you were expecting to see him on the bus?'

It seemed to Martin that a decade passed before she replied. On her answer, would hang his whole future, his life, his everything. His destiny lay in the kernel of one small word. He watched her biting delicately at one corner of her lip.

Finally, she turned her head slowly in the direction of her interrogator.

'I know nothing about him at all,' she said in a voice scarcely above a whisper.

'But you have confessed to your criminal acts. You have admitted your part in the conspiracy to aid the traitor woman Zwehl.'

'That is true. But this man was not involved. I had never seen him before and I know nothing of him.'

Martin felt like a computer into which too much conflicting data has been fed and which is unable to come up with any sort of rational answer.

The two basic facts which jutted out like sharp rocks were that Anna Schmidt had confessed her part in the enterprise, but notwithstanding was covering up for him. Could he, however, be really sure of this when he did not even know what she had been told about *his* part in the affair? Was it not just possible that she had never been told of his rôle? After all, now that he came to think of it, she had not needed to know his instructions in order to carry out her own in that event she could be telling the truth as she believed it to be. She really did not know anything about him. He really was a complete stranger to her; a fortuitous bus companion. That, however, still left one indisputable fact. The fact that she herself was now in the greatest possible danger. A self-confessed spy in a country obsessively suspicious on the subject.

As he now looked at her, he was filled with a desire to snatch off her dark glasses, to fathom the expression which they successfully eclipsed, to see for the first time her eyes, those proverbial mirrors of the soul.

Instead, he could only observe her individual features, welded together in a mask of numb despair.

'You realise,' the interpreter was translating, 'that your only hope is to tell the whole truth now. Lying will help neither of you.'

She shrugged. 'I've given you the whole truth,' she said wearily. 'If I knew anything about this man, I'd tell you.'

Martin gazed at her with a feeling of overwhelming respect, tinged with raging despair. Respect for her staunch refusal to be brow-beaten into incriminating him: despair on account of her grim plight which he was powerless to influence. He felt like someone standing impotently on the edge of a bog watching a victim sink slowly towards oblivion.

Furthermore, the whole episode acquired the qualities of a chilling nightmare since he was quite unable to divine the purpose of her apparently quixotic behaviour.

By God, if anyone deserved to spend the next twenty years in a Bulgarian dungeon, it was Peacock! Peacock who blithely despatched his minions on errands such as this. What right had he to deal so lightly in human life and liberty! To him, Anna Schmidt was an expendable pawn. He did not have to see her, as Martin now did, after the trap into which she had walked had been remorselessly sprung.

Bald-head said something to the wardress who stood up and touched Anna Schmidt on the shoulder. She rose and without a glance in Martin's direction disappeared through the door she had entered by. Had it not been for his awareness that three pairs of eyes were watching him intently, Martin felt that he must have even more clearly revealed the sense of desolation which suddenly took possession of his body like a physical ague. He had never experienced anything like it before.

'Colonel Petrov asks if you are feeling quite well,' the interpreter said, his voice seeming to come from far off.

Martin nodded. He must pull himself together.

'I've been up several hours and not yet had breakfast,' he said.

Bald-head spoke for several seconds. Then getting up abruptly from the table, he stalked from the room.

'I think you will just have time for a cup of coffee before the bus goes,' the interpreter said with a wisp of a smile. 'You can find your way to the lobby?'

Martin stared at him disbelievingly. Was he really being told that the ordeal was over and that life took up where it had left off ... was it two weeks ... six months ... or twenty years ago?

He had lost all sense of the hour, but now glancing at his watch saw that it was a quarter to nine. It was difficult to recall a time which had not been spent in that great bare, subterranean room. And yet his watch was trying to persuade him that it was only the last half-hour of his life which had actually been passed there. He had started out as the affronted innocent and ended as a numbered, bewildered and frightened man. And who should know better than he what good cause he had for fear! He might have been invited to rejoin the bus, but that did not mean danger was past.

As he reached the top of the stairs, he saw a number of his fellow passengers wandering about the lobby examining the pictures on the walls, the sparsely filled rack of postcards and the trivia to which people are wont to give rapt attention in a strange place when they have time on their hands. He could see others strolling on the terrace outside the main entrance.

Martin was still bemusedly glancing about him when Rogov came bustling up.

'Please come, your breakfast is ready. We leave in ten minutes.'

Martin followed him into a large dining-room, now empty apart from the bus crew sitting together at a table over in one corner. Mr Gursan was standing talking to them. Rogov led him to a freshly laid place at one of the tables and hurried off to the service door.

Though he had no appetite, he knew that he ought to eat something and spread a thick slice of bread with butter and raspberry jam. He was half-way through it, when a waitress brought him a platter of cheese, a boiled egg and some coffee. He gulped the coffee down thirstily and poured himself a second cup, and was just giving his attention to the egg when Mr Gursan came across to the table.

'It is good, the Bulgarian breakfast, is it not?'

Martin nodded. 'Very good.'

'But you very nearly not have it?'

'I was held up.'

'They want to ask you questions about Fräulein Schmidt, yes?' he asked keenly, at the same time pulling out a chair and sitting down.

'Yes,' Martin replied bleakly, without caring whether it was wise to satisfy Mr Gursan's curiosity. He still felt Mr Gursan was someone who could be trusted, even though this was based on nothing stronger than an instinct, which Peacock would certainly condemn as dangerously unreliable.

'I knew she was not ill,' Mr Gursan went on with a gesture of impatience. 'She is in trouble with police, yes?'

'It appears so.'

'And you were able to help them?'

'I wasn't able to tell them anything at all. I had nothing to tell them. I'd never set eyes on her before I got on the bus.'

'But they thought otherwise, yes?'

'I suppose they must have thought so. But they were wrong.'

'What is she in trouble about with the police?'

Mr Gursan's questions were asked with a keenness which he did nothing to try and mask, and Martin decided he either had to take him into his complete confidence or to rebuff his curiosity. Despite his appearance of trustworthiness, however, he did not yet feel ready to make an ally out of him.

'I've no idea. They didn't let on.'

Mr Gursan pursed his lips thoughtfully. 'There is something strange happening . . .' he murmured, and fell into silence.

'Why are you so interested in Fräulein Schmidt?' Martin inquired. After all, two could play at inquisitiveness, and he certainly no longer felt himself bound by Peacock's rule book.

Mr Gursan looked up sharply.

'A pretty girl disappears and it is said the police have detained her; is that not a matter of interest? Especially when the pretty girl is a fellow passenger on the bus? Who would not be interested? We are all interested and you are the one to tell us what has happened.'

'Except that I'm not, because I don't know any more than the rest of you. I was questioned by the police only because I happened to have been sitting next to her. It could just as well have been another passenger who had that seat.'

For several seconds, Mr Gursan looked at him as though he was an interesting new specimen in a zoo. Then he got up and, patting Martin's arm, said good-humouredly, 'Enjoy your breakfast, my friend.'

Martin had just finished his meal when Rogov stuck his head through the door.

'Please come now, the bus is leaving.'

As Martin passed through the lobby, he cast a quick glance down the staircase leading to the basement, but no sign of life came from below. He wondered whether Anna Schmidt was still on the premises or whether she was now on her way back to a prison cell in Sofia. And then suddenly, as though a spring catch had been released in his brain, he began to wonder a lot of other things.

Why had they taken the trouble to bring Anna Schmidt from Sofia to this small mountain resort? Why, in fact, had they chosen this as the place to interrogate him and arrange the confrontation with her when it must have been much easier to hold it in the capital? They could easily have stopped him getting on the bus first thing that morning. It was odd! Something strange was happening, as Mr Gursan had murmured only a few minutes ago. And where exactly did *he* fit in?

And the note warning him against catching Anna Schmidt's cold! The events of the past hour had chased it completely from his mind. What on earth had it meant? And more important, did it still have any meaning? Was Anna Schmidt's behaviour at the recent interrogation meant to be construed as a determination on her part not to give him her cold, i.e., not to embroil him in her own trouble? But the note had been passed to him before her arrest had taken place, which clearly indicated that the writer knew what was in store for her. Presumably he must also have thought there was a danger that she might try and pass on her cold to him.

The bus's horn brought him out of his reverie and he quickened his pace across the terrace and down the winding path which led to the road.

As he mentally surveyed the wreckage of what had once been Peacock's plan, one fact stood out a mile. There was nothing left of it. Nothing!

He climbed into the bus, which was waiting to go, and made his way back to his seat. Half-way to it he suddenly slowed in his tracks as his gaze fell on the seat next to his.

Sitting there and looking unconcernedly out of the window was a dark-haired girl. What was more, she was wearing a pair of sun-glasses which were the twin of Anna Schmidt's.

CHAPTER SIX

To jump a few hours forward, on this same day that Martin had a snatched breakfast at Borovets, Peacock had a leisurely lunch at his club in St James's. He usually managed to get across there for lunch twice a week and his visits always followed the same pattern. He would have a glass of medium dry sherry in the bar and exchange a few urbane remarks with anyone there whom he happened to know. But he seldom stopped for more than ten minutes in the bar and never had a second sherry.

He would then make his way to the dining-room where he always had smoked trout and the hot joint with two green vegetables, but no potatoes. This would be washed down by a glass of club claret. Rarely did he have anything else, though there were occasions when he fancied some fresh fruit and would carefully select an apple or a pear from the basket which would be placed before him with the deference of a votive offering.

Afterwards he would go upstairs to the reading room, help himself to a large cup of black coffee, collect a number of magazines and settle down in one of the capacious black leather arm-chairs.

In the final ten minutes before returning to the office, he liked to cast his mind over the whole range of current operations, from those still in the planning stage to those which had been blue-printed weeks, if not months, before and which were now in the process of execution.

On this particular day, having finished his coffee and having cursorily read both the *Spectator* and the *New Statesman*, he gave his mind exclusively to Martin Ainsworth and the assignment which he had undertaken.

Though he recognised the necessity, and had appeared to make a virtue of it to Martin, he was never entirely happy about using other than professionally trained staff on such operations. Indeed, he personally never did unless forced to do so by the sort of circumstances which had caused him to enlist Martin's aid, but it chilled him to think that a whole intricately planned operation could go awry all because a child caught chicken pox and passed it on to her father.

It was not that he doubted Martin's intelligence or resourcefulness, just that he lacked the mental stamina which training alone can develop. Just as the seasoned professional has the edge over the gifted amateur in almost every field of sport, so it was in his shadowy realm of activity.

Today was the crucial day in the operation and he was impatient for the reports which should be coming in at this very moment. So far he had heard nothing beyond the fact that the bus had left Munich on time with Martin and Anna Schmidt on board and had reached Zagreb without event.

Brian Hart, his man in Munich, was one of the ablest the department had, though it was sometimes necessary to remind him that he had superiors in London who liked to be kept in touch with what was going on. He had a tendency to become elusive when an operation of which he had field control was under way and only report when it was all over.

Peacock jacked himself out of his chair and went downstairs to collect his hat (a bowler from Lockes) and umbrella. Eager though he was to get back and find out what news had come through from Hart, he walked down St James's Street and across the park in an unhurried fashion. Self-control was a facet of character by which he set great store and in his job it was particularly important to be able to keep under control such human emotions as impatience, excitement and disappointment.

He hung up his hat and umbrella in the closet next to his room which he then entered via his secretary's.

'Anything from Brian Hart?' he inquired as he passed through the connecting door.

'Yes, on your desk,' she replied, watching his back disappear. He was quite one of the coldest fish she had ever worked for. There was, however, nothing you could take exception to in him save that his arteries appeared to be filled with iced water in place of blood. His last secretary had been transferred to other duties after an emotional outburst which had left him indifferent and her prostrate.

It happened when he had required her for the third time in three days to retype a long report. On the final occasion, each of them was feeling tired and she had cried out, 'You don't like me, Mr Peacock, do you?'

He had looked at her impassively for several seconds before replying, 'I neither like, nor do I dislike, you. I'm merely concerned with whether you do your work properly. Now kindly go and type that bloody report again.'

Peacock sat down at his desk and, putting on his spectacles, flipped through the memos and cables, looking for one from the Munich office. It was near the bottom of the pile and read:

'Ainsworth having a bumpy ride as foreseen and feared. But plan intact.'

Peacock read it through a second time. It was a typical Hart effort, but the vital part of the message was contained in the last three words ... *But plan intact.*

He permitted himself a small purr of satisfaction.

CHAPTER SEVEN

From Borovets the road swung downhill in a series of sharp bends. Ali was at the wheel and handled the bus with all the skill of a steeple-chasing jockey determined to beat the course record.

Revived by breakfast and seemingly stimulated by the driving, the Persians chatted among themselves with greater animation than ever, the girl with the unquenchable laugh almost rolling off her seat every time one of her compatriots addressed her.

Dr and Frau Springer sat in customary aloofness in so far as it was possible to be aloof under such conditions. Near them Fräulein Benzl was unfolding a fresh map and gazing out eagerly for landmarks as the bus waltzed its way towards the floor of the valley.

A bit farther back, Mr Gursan was sitting very still with his hands folded in his lap, staring straight ahead of him in an apparent brown study.

All this Martin took in, as he once more tried to make sense out of what had happened.

In the first place one thing which was certain was that the girl in the seat next to him was not Anna Schmidt. She was about the same age, she had the same dark hair and the same pale complexion and, of course, the identical glasses. He judged her, however, to be a bit shorter than Anna Schmidt.

But who was she? And what was she doing on the bus? After all that had happened it seemed inconceivable that she was Paula Zwehl! But how could she be Paula Zwehl! It was less than an hour ago that the man called Colonel Petrov had accused him of coming to the country to rescue the person he referred to as 'the traitor Paula Zwehl'. And if it was not Anna Schmidt and it was not Paula Zwehl, who was it? Was this some ace which Peacock had had up his sleeve the whole time ... Was this the girl he had to pretend was Anna Schmidt of Munich against all doubters? He just did not know. He almost did not care. *Almost*; that is, except for his sense of personal survival which was still strong enough to keep his mind probing what might lie ahead like a restless radar scanner.

But it was the utter failure to make sense out of events which really paralysed him. He felt completely and hopelessly adrift. He was without compass, sextant or rudder and there were not even moon or stars to give him a bearing.

All he could do was sit silent and find relief in every mile that passed without further trauma.

The girl at his side suddenly turned and said in an urgent whisper, 'We must be very careful. Things have gone wrong. There is much danger.'

She spoke in German, but Martin's was not sufficiently good to tell him whether this was her native tongue. He gave her a fleeting smile of incomprehension, but made no reply.

'You understand?' she asked fiercely.

'I understand German, but I don't know what it is you're saying.'

58

'We must be very careful,' she repeated. 'There is danger all around.'

Martin gave her the sort of smile reserved for humouring harmless lunatics, but otherwise made no response and as abruptly as she had begun talking to him, she turned her head away and went back to looking out of the window.

Whether she really might be the prize in the Peacock planned operation or whether she was a plant of the local secret police, he was satisfied he had played it the right way. That is to say, he had given nothing away. Moreover, it had not needed anyone to tell him that there was danger all around. He must certainly keep his eye on the girl when they stopped for a break. It was possible that he might learn something about her then.

The bus had meanwhile rejoined the main road, though only to leave it again. This time to detour through a number of small farming villages. They very much resembled villages anywhere in western Europe, save for the inevitable party banners and portraits which adorned all the civic buildings.

Such traffic as there was consisted, for the most part, of dilapidated trucks laden with produce. One convoy of trucks were stacked to a crazy height with crates of hens, whose feathers appeared to be almost being blown off their bodies by the force of the wind.

About the middle of the morning, they reached Plovdiv, which the guide announced as the second largest town in Bulgaria. Martin braced himself for trouble, but in the event nothing worse befell them than getting stuck behind an enormous lorry and trailer which had broken down. Ali dealt with this situation by driving up on to the pavement and back on to the road between a variety of scattered obstacles, to the accompaniment of delighted noises from his compatriots. Fifteen minutes later, they were once more in open country and shortly after one o'clock arrived at a town called Haskovo.

'Haskovo, where we will have our lunch,' Rogov intoned, 'is an important economic and cultural centre.'

If Martin had not had other things on his mind, he would have asked what was important about it *culturally*. It had long irritated him the way that word was currently overworked in the communist countries and was accorded a pretentious solemnity it did not deserve. As it was he gazed out on a scene of half-finished new buildings and peeling old ones and saw nothing remotely cultural in his line of vision, save for a cinema advertising what was clearly another epic in the struggle against imperialism. A line of husky young men and women were shown sternly brushing aside the clawings of some mafia-type looking men whose faces wore twisted snarls of fury and frustration.

The bus came to a halt in a square, on one side of which was a modern hotel.

'Here is where we take our lunch,' Rogov said with simple pride, as though he expected a round of applause.

As Martin got out, Mr Gursan, who had hung back, turned and waited for him to catch up.

'You're a lucky man, eh?' he said breezily as Martin drew level with him.

'Lucky? In what way am I lucky?' Martin inquired in a not too friendly tone.

'You have another beautiful girl sitting beside you. Is that not luck? I have only the old German lady since Munich.'

Martin felt a sudden tingle of excitement. Was this the great test? Was this the moment for which he had been carefully rehearsed? Was this warm, dusty town square in eastern Bulgaria the divinely chosen scene of enactment of his journey? But too much had gone wrong; too many things which he did not begin to understand had occurred, for him to be able to play his part with any conviction.

'Another?' he said stupidly.

Mr Gursan looked at him sharply. 'You are not thinking that it is still Fräulein Schmidt beside you?'

'Oh, I see what you mean,' Martin said trying to recover himself. 'I didn't quite understand what you meant.'

How could he ever have thought to try and pretend that he supposed he was still sitting next to Anna Schmidt. And to Mr Gursan of all people, who had shown such a lively interest in what had happened to her. He was so confused, he really did not know where he was. It was like living through a nightmare in which every object reacts with hostility towards one.

'Who is your new companion?' Mr Gursan went on.

'I've no idea. We've not had any conversation.'

'No?' Mr Gursan's tone indicated his disbelief of this statement.

'She is Bulgarian perhaps?'

'I've no idea.'

'She resembles the other girl, I think; yes?'

'I've not noticed.'

Mr Gursan shot him an amused glance, as though he was enjoying Martin's discomfiture.

'You will excuse please, I have something to do,' Mr Gursan said as they were about to enter the hotel, and disappeared across the street and into a shop.

As Martin stood there for a moment, a man and a woman came out speaking English. They got into a car with G.B. plates and drove off with a throaty roar. It was all he could do not to rush after them and beg a lift to wherever they were going. He felt like a shipwrecked man who sees the possibility of rescue slip through his fingers.

The hotel dining-room was full, but he was able to find a table to himself. He sat down and abstractedly drank the soup which was placed before him. In another four hours or so, the bus should have entered Turkey and his troubles would be over. He would be out of danger.

He glanced round the room to check on his fellow passengers. This was something which had now become routine with him. Everyone was present save Mr Gursan and the girl in Anna Schmidt's seat. He had not noticed where she went on getting out of the bus.

Dr and Frau Springer were sitting alone away from the rest. Frau Springer was talking earnestly to her husband who was listening to her with an expression of judicial boredom.

Martin looked up to see the girl enter the dining-room. She stood for a moment gazing about her and then came straight over to his table and sat down.

As soon as the waitress had brought her soup and departed again, she said in a jerky whisper, 'You don't have to pretend, I know everything. It is all right to talk to me. We must be very careful, though.'

'I might understand better, if you told me who you were. As it is ...'

'I am Paula Zwehl. Ah, I see you know my name!' she exclaimed.

'I heard it mentioned by someone this morning,' Martin said cautiously. 'A police officer at Borovets suggested that I knew a person of that name.'

'And you denied it, yes?'

'I denied it.'

'Good.'

'Because I *didn't* know anyone of that name,' he added firmly.

'You are clever. But we must trust each other,' she said, while scanning his face intently as though trying to count the pores in his skin. 'There are enemies even on the bus.'

'What do you want me to do?'

'Tell me, what are your instructions?'

'I'm afraid I've no idea what you're talking about,' he replied stolidly.

She made an impatient gesture with her hand.

'You must trust me,' she hissed. 'There is great danger, if you will not help me.' She put out a hand and rested it briefly on Martin's arm. 'Please!'

Of one thing he was quite certain, this girl was not Paula Zwehl. It was inconceivable that while he was being interrogated in the hotel basement about his part in the plot to rescue her—the traitor Paula Zwehl, Colonel Petrov had stigmatised her—Paula Zwehl herself was outside waiting to join the bus. If she was anywhere, she would have been in a prison cell. And if this girl was not Paula Zwehl, then she could only be an agent of the secret police put there to try and trap him. It was about the only thing which made sense. A clumsy, naïve attempt it was at that, for how could they possibly have thought he would be taken in by such a transparent trick. But if they knew it would be that obvious, why had they attempted it? Martin's effort at rationalising the girl's presence came to a jolting halt.

A small sound caused him to glance at her. To his dismay, he saw that she was quietly crying. Almost immediately she pushed her chair back from the table and hurried out of the dining-room, leaving her food uneaten.

Martin cast an embarrassed glance round the room to see whether anyone had noticed, but it did not appear so. The Persians were digging into an enormous pile of cherries like a flock of eager starlings and the remainder were either bent over their food or sitting back in attitudes of quiescent boredom, waiting to be told the next move. As usual, Hans and Ali and Toni appeared to be eating their way through a quite different and much larger meal than that served to their passengers. Martin had observed this early on in the journey and assumed it to be one of the perks of the job.

Satisfied that no one's attention had been attracted, he finished what was in front of him and left the dining-room. There was no reason why anyone should have noticed since the girl had been sitting with her back to most people and her dark glasses had hidden her tears from anyone not seeing her face at close quarters.

Martin walked out into the square and stood in the sunshine. He reckoned it could not be much more than another fifty miles to the frontier, that is provided there were not any further detours. Moreover, the road should be through flattish country which should make for fast driving. He looked at his watch. If they got away by half past two, they must reach the frontier by half past four at the latest. That gave them several hours of daylight to spare. After the shock of events at Borovets, the morning had passed with unexpected calm, though this had done nothing to diminish his sensation of being strapped to a time bomb. Everything that had happened since he had entered Bulgaria eighteen hours before had confirmed the feeling and it was not until he was safely out of the country that he was going to be able to relax.

He did not know whether it was the genial effect of the sun or the rather good lunch, but he was aware that his sense of fear had grown less. His confidence was once more on an upward trend. It could be, he decided, that it was no more than the upsurge of confidence of the lonely sniper who repulses a heavy attack on his position. Further attacks are possible, even probable, but what has been done once can be done a second time—with increased confidence.

Other passengers were beginning to come out of the hotel and he watched Hans and Ali stride purposefully across to the bus and go to the back where the engine was situated. Ali fetched some tools and there was a sound of hammering.

Martin strolled over to see what was happening. Hans' hands were covered in oil when he withdrew his arms from the engine. Ali handed him a large rag and then went back to the tool compartment near the front of the bus.

'Anything wrong?' Martin inquired.

'A washer gone.'

'Is that going to delay us?'

'About half an hour.'

Hans' head disappeared under the cowling again and Martin walked away.

Well, half an hour was not too bad, though he could have done without the wait. Fortunately, both drivers seemed to be conversant with the mechanical whims of the huge, filthily dirty engine which roared away at the rear and there was no reason to doubt their ability to put this right.

As matters turned out, however, it was an hour and a quarter before they were on the move again, by which time everyone, save the ebullient Persians, was fretting at the delay. And when finally they did get off, it was to be held up for a further twenty minutes at a level crossing on the outskirts of the town.

The girl next to Martin sat huddled in what he took to be reproachful silence and he was content to accept that. From time to time she half lifted herself out of her seat and scanned the backs of the heads in the rows in front. It was almost as if she was trying to catch someone's attention, save that when anyone did happen to look back in their direction she quickly sank down into her seat.

They were passing through a flat cultivated landscape which had groups of workers toiling in the fields. There were both men and women and old and young.

'Here much tobacco is grown,' Toni announced, in the absence of Mr Rogov who had not reappeared on the bus after lunch.

There were a number of small villages with roses growing wild everywhere and storks nesting on rooftops.

'This part of Bulgaria is famous for its rose growing,' Toni went on. 'You have all heard of attar of roses. This is where it comes from.'

They had been travelling for just over an hour and were about two miles past a particularly picturesque village when a terrible clattering noise came from the engine. Hans brought the bus to an immediate halt and, accompanied by Ali, got out to inspect. It was several minutes before Ali came to the door and spoke to Toni, who then made an announcement.

'I am afraid, ladies and gentlemen, that we have a repair to make. It will take about two hours. You may get out if you wish but please do not go far from the bus.'

There was an immediate outbreak of chatter, as people stood up and stretched and looked at their watches.

Mr Gursan wandered back to Martin's seat.

'It will be dark before we reach the frontier,' he observed in a tone which seemed designed to draw comment.

'How far *is* the frontier?'

'Twenty-five kilometres.'

'And Istanbul from there?'

'Four hours driving.' He gave Martin a quizzical look. 'You do not like this delay I think?'

'I never welcome delays.'

'But some are worse than others, yes?'

Martin shrugged. 'They're all a nuisance.'

'And your friend beside you, what does she think?'

'You'd better ask her.'

The girl had been paying no obvious attention to their conversation and had given no sign that she understood English.

In the pause which followed, Martin decided that there was no reason why he should not retaliate against Mr Gursan by asking a few questions himself. He still had not fathomed the cause of the Turk's curiosity about him and his seat companion, though he had observed that he showed a general interest in most of the passengers. Mr Gursan, in fact, was the great attacher. Whenever the bus stopped and they all got out, he was invariably to be seen attaching himself to one group or another. It was possible, therefore, that his curiosity was no more than that of the naturally inquisitive person.

'The couple sitting just behind you,' Martin said, 'they intrigue me. They don't look the sort of people to travel on buses. Do you know who they are?'

'Dr and Frau Springer,' Mr Gursan replied, lowering his head so that they would not hear his voice.

'Where do they come from?'

'They are from Cologne.'

'And what is Doctor Springer a doctor of?'

'He is not a medicine doctor. More I do not know.'

'And Frau Springer? She's a striking looking woman.'

'Ah, so you think so too! She is very strong personality, yes?'

'I would think so.'

'You know her?'

'I've never spoken to her.' After a slight pause, he added, 'Why do you think I know everyone on the bus?'

'I don't know,' Mr Gursan replied unabashed, 'I just ask.'

'Well, I don't know her or anyone else. I'm travelling alone.'

'Yes, you have already explained you are on your holidays.' Mr Gursan's tone had the merest sardonic inflection and Martin glanced at him sharply. His expression, however, remained impassively benevolent. 'I go and see how they get on with the reparation.' He strolled off down the aisle of the bus and got out.

Meanwhile Martin had been noticing that the girl beside

him had been exhibiting signs of growing restiveness. She constantly glanced anxiously at her watch and was behaving like someone who realised she was going to be late for an important appointment. She made no further efforts, however, to embroil his interest and he certainly had no intention of encouraging her to do so.

Accordingly, shortly after Mr Gursan had left his side, Martin also got up and went to see how the repair work was progressing.

Hans and Ali had an audience of about a dozen at the rear of the bus, and Ali was providing his usual wise-cracking commentary for their benefit. Portions of the innards of the engine lay on a tarpaulin beside the baggage trailer.

'Ah, my English friend,' he cried out on spotting Martin among the group of watchers. 'Not so very fine, eh! We should have English bus, eh? Very fine buses in England. English buses never go wrong, eh?'

Martin grinned under the barrage of innocent banter.

'How is the repair coming along?' he asked, while Ali wiped some of the excess oil off himself with a filthy rag.

'It is big job,' Ali replied, the corners of his mouth turned down in gallic despair. His expression brightened. 'But Hans is very fine mechanic.'

All that could be seen of Hans were his legs and his bottom, the rest of him being inside the engine casing.

'You'll be able to do it all right?'

'We do it,' Ali said in the tone of a general instilling confidence in his anxious troops. 'Never fear, Istanbul will still be there when we arrive.'

With this encouraging prophecy, he joined Hans head first inside the black cavern occupied by the engine.

Mr Gursan came up beside Martin.

'I do not think,' he said judicially, 'that we shall be ready to go until it is dark. That is your view, too?'

Martin gazed up at the sky. Although it was still perfectly light, there were indications of gathering dusk in the sky towards the east.

'I suppose it'll be dark in about another hour,' he remarked casually.

Darkness came, however, in less than that. The labourers in the fields packed up and evaporated, but Hans and Ali still worked at the engine, though now by the light of torches held by volunteers.

From time to time a car would pass, usually bearing German plates. The Germans, Martin reflected, were again the predominant holiday-makers all over Southern Europe. Sometimes a transcontinental lorry with trailer would thunder by, its huge black shape seemingly full of menace in the gathering gloom.

But no one paid their broken-down bus or its passengers any attention. No other vehicle stopped, none of the labourers from the fields came over to see what was the matter. It was as though they were in strict quarantine and everyone knew it.

It was nearly eight o'clock before Hans and Ali put their tools away, cleaned themselves as best they could and announced that all was well.

At a jab of the starter, the engine gave a satisfactory roar and settled back into its customary idling rattle. Hans took the driver's seat and with a ragged cheer from the Persians they resumed their journey.

The girl beside Martin who had been curled up with a scarf right over her head when he returned to the bus, now sat up with a start and peered at her watch. She seemed to be in a state of suppressed agitation.

Martin reckoned they had covered about half the distance to the frontier when it all happened.

They were travelling along a straight bit of road with trees on both sides and no sign of human habitation when quite suddenly a red lantern was being swung across their path about fifty yards ahead. Martin who had happened to be gazing in that direction thought at first it was a level crossing, but then in the bus's headlights he saw a man swinging the lantern. A man in uniform.

Hans brought the bus to a halt only a couple of yards from where the guard was standing. He slid open the driver's window and stuck his head out to speak to him. A few seconds later he clambered out of his seat and went to the door of the bus. Standing on the bottom step, he had a further conversation with the guard who had come round to that side of the bus.

It appeared that Hans was protesting, but it was impossible to hear what was passing between them.

For a full minute, no one else spoke, even the Persians being stilled into silence by the sudden chill of dramatic happening.

As for Martin, he felt himself sitting in rigid fear. He was aware of the girl next to him standing up and gazing wildly in the direction of Hans and his hidden interrogator.

Abruptly Hans turned and faced them. Taking the microphone from Toni, he said in a stony voice devoid of emotion, 'Will you please have your passports ready for inspection.'

'Is this the frontier?' someone called out.

'No. It is a special check.'

'A special check? What for?' The speaker sounded indignant.

'Please have your passports ready,' Hans repeated, this time with a touch of authority in his tone. 'The check won't take long if you do as you're asked.'

'They suspect something,' Martin heard one of the Germans in front of him say. 'It's something to do with one of the passengers . . .' another voice added in an anxious tone.

'No, no, they can't . . .' This time it was Martin's companion who spoke. She was still standing up and leaning over the back of the seat in front. She was shaking her head in disbelief. 'No . . . no, they mustn't . . .'

Martin tapped her arm.

'I'd sit down and try and keep calm,' he said. 'It'll be better for us all if you do.'

She turned towards him and spat out something in a language he did not understand. Then she fell back into her seat and gripped the arm-rests as though to defy anyone's efforts to remove her.

Meanwhile the guard had stepped into the bus and was standing just inside the door. He gave them a perfunctory salute and said something in Bulgarian.

After the salute, his right hand came to rest ostentatiously on the butt of his revolver. As he stood there motionless in the dimly lit interior of the bus with its air of shadowy gloom, it flashed through Martin's mind that he represented a figure of nemesis to each one of them. There was complete silence: they were like characters out of a J. B. Priestley play, behaving in a mundane way one minute and then suddenly transported into a strange timeless realm of no dimensions.

The spell was broken when the guard moved. Pulling a flashlight out of one pocket he held out his hand for the nearest passenger's passport. He examined it carefully in the light of his torch, then with dramatic suddenness turned the beam on to the face of the owner of the passport. The woman concerned let out a gasp as one hand went up to shield her eyes. The next moment her passport lay in her lap and the guard was going through a similar routine with the passenger next to her.

He had examined about eight passports before it dawned on Martin that he was taking considerably longer over women's than over men's. As the realisation of this came to him, he glanced at the girl in the seat beside him. She was sitting bolt upright, watching events with an expression of frozen disbelief.

The guard was working faster now and in a couple of minutes he would reach them. For Martin, this was the moment of decision. He had no idea what was happening and was aware only of approaching crisis. Was this the moment for him to nail his colours to the mast and declare resolutely that his companion was none of the things they were going to suggest? But what were they going to suggest? And anyway how could he support her when he knew less than nothing about her? She had asked for his trust earlier and he had prevaricated. Now it was too late. Had he journeyed all this distance to look the other way when the crunch came? It seemed so.

He noticed that Frau Springer's passport appeared to excite more attention than most others, but when the guard played the beam of his torch full on to her face, she just gazed ahead of her in icy disdain.

The silence in the bus was still almost complete, and was broken only by an occasional whisper exchanged between the Persians, who sitting at the front had been among the first to undergo the ordeal.

Martin watched Fräulein Benzl hand the guard her passport and fix him with a hard stare while he turned its pages. When the bright shaft of light was thrown on her face, Martin was taken aback to see an expression of cold hatred.

The guard turned and murmured something to Hans who was immediately behind him. Hans, who had a grim look on his face, shook his head and they moved on.

They were now only two rows from Martin's seat and he was able to study the guard's face more closely. He was a man of medium build with prominent cheekbones, a firm, sensual mouth and a chin which broadened when all his other features ordained that it should have fallen away to a point. His expression was one of arrogant self-confidence. The expression to be seen on the faces of the élite police in any country which goes in for the breed. His eyes were ever watchful.

He now came up beside Martin's seat and put out his hand

for his passport.

'English?' he asked, as though practising his pronunciation of the word.

Martin nodded and held his breath. But what had he got to be worried about? He had done nothing wrong. Nothing that anyone could prove, anyway. If they had had anything on him, they would not have let him leave Borovets. Borovets! It seemed a hundred years and three million miles away. He braced himself against the blinding assault of the torch and was aware of Mr Gursan observing him with steady interest. When it came, he blinked and felt himself licking his lips in guilty fear, but then the light was flicked off and his passport was back in his hand.

The guard stretched across to take the girl's. Her hand trembled violently as she gave it to him. She said something in a low voice and in a language which Martin did not recognise but assumed to be Bulgarian. Her tone was nervously vehement. The guard said nothing, but went on examining the passport with studied deliberation.

Then abruptly he slipped it into his pocket and shone the torch straight into her face. She recoiled as though she had been physically struck and let out a great cry. The guard spoke sharply and put out a hand to seize her arm, but she withdrew from his reach.

He then spoke again in the same tone while she stared at him in a mixture of anger and frustration.

He motioned Martin to leave his seat and, when he did so, leant across and took firmly hold of the girl's arm. He pulled her into the gangway and pushed her ahead of him towards the front of the bus, while everyone watched in shocked bewilderment.

It was Fräulein Benzl's voice which broke the awed silence. As Hans passed by her seat, she said, 'Why is this girl being removed from the bus?'

'The police wish to question her,' Hans replied uneasily.

'Why?'

'Her papers are not in order.'

'What is she supposed to have done?'

Hans glared. 'I don't know and I haven't asked because I shouldn't be told.'

'What nationality is she?' Fräulein Benzl persisted.

'Bulgarian, according to her passport.'

He hurried after the guard who was waiting impatiently by

the entrance, one hand still gripping the girl's arm.

The guard muttered something and Martin caught the word 'bleiben'. Hans said, 'No one is to leave the bus.'

'What's happening now?' someone asked anxiously.

'He is not satisfied until he has searched the baggage trailer,' Hans explained and then got out of the bus behind the guard.

Immediately everyone began talking at once, as tension was released like a dam of water. Martin, however, was hardly aware of the noise of anxious chatter as his swirling thoughts dissolved like morning mist to disclose clearly the path he knew he must take. This time he must act—and act now. He had to find out what was going on.

Getting up from his seat, he walked quickly down the aisle and opened the bus door. It was only as he was doing so that Toni put out a protesting hand.

'No one may leave the bus,' she said. 'Police orders.'

Ignoring her, he jumped out and slammed the door behind him, vaguely aware of the fresh silence which his precipitate departure had brought about.

The light from the interior of the bus hardly penetrated the darkness outside, but he moved out of its meagre range and quickened his pace to where he could see the reflected glow of the guard's torch. Somewhere at the back of his mind he persuaded himself that his fellow passengers were probably thinking he was either mad or the quixotically chivalrous English gentleman. Though why any part of his mind should have concerned itself at that moment with the impression his conduct was creating was something which it would have taken a psychiatrist to dredge from his sub-conscious.

He saw that the doors of the luggage trailer were open and that it was Hans who was shining the torch into the interior, or rather on to the solid wall of suitcases which reached to the front. The guard still had a tight hold of the girl, who was now gagged.

Martin's immediate impression was that they were going to shut her away with the baggage. Before he had a chance to say anything, Hans swung round and shone the torch straight at him. At the same moment the guard drew his revolver and pointed it at Martin's stomach.

There was something sufficiently menacing in the gesture to cause Martin to hurl himself sideways, duck and run. As he did so, a shot rang out. He did not hear the whine of the bullet and assumed it to be well wide. There was a grass verge on the other side of the road and he ran along this for about twenty-five yards before plunging into the field which lay on his left.

Bushes caught at his trousers as he fought his way across soft, dry ground. Exhausted he flung himself down and lay as flat as he could. It was now that he realised he was in one of the vast fields of cultivated roses which covered the landscape in that area. As his eyes grew accustomed to the dark he could see the serried rows of bushes stretching away on either side of him.

Raising himself up slightly he peered over the top of the nearest bush. He could see the dim outline of the bus about a hundred yards away. But hard though he listened he was unable to hear a sound. It seemed that they had made no attempt to pursue him.

This struck him as odd. It could mean only one thing, that they had not the time to waste. While he was so thinking, he heard the engine come to life and a second later the bus pulled away.

He got into a kneeling position and watched it go. For several seconds after the sound had died away he could see the receding tail-light. Then that, too, vanished and he was alone.

He stood up and brushed himself down with his hands. Next he looked at his watch and saw that it was nearly nine o'clock. From the surrounding stillness and absence of any sign of life, it felt more like 3 a.m.

Considering his predicament, it was strange how calm he felt. Now he really was thrown back on to his own resources. His situation reminded him of something he had not thought about in twenty years. Night patrols when he was in the army during the last war. He recalled how much better the country lads had been on them than those bred in towns. He had always picked the farmers' boys to go out on patrol with him. They enjoyed an intuitive communion with the dark, silent countryside, whereas the town lads were jumpy and nervous—and, most fatal of all, noisy. He himself had relished exercising the basic skills which night patrol work called for.

Quietly he made his way back to the road, then along the verge to where the bus had been. Before deciding on his next move, he wanted to see whether there were any indications as to what happened to the girl.

Also he was puzzled about the guard. He had not seen any other vehicle leave the area and yet the guard must have had a car parked somewhere in the vicinity. Supposing he was still around! Martin halted in his tracks and stepped down into the dry ditch and lay there while he thought.

While he was doing so, he heard a car approaching from behind. Raising his head, he peered cautiously down the road to see headlights about a quarter of a mile away. He pressed himself into the bottom of the ditch until the moment of the car passing, then quickly raised himself to take advantage of a sight of the lit-up road ahead.

But he saw nothing and a minute later the night was once more silent and empty.

He reached the point opposite to where the bus had been parked and, crouching low, made a quick dash across the road to the sanctuary of the ditch on the other side.

For half a minute he just lay there, listening for any sounds, in particular for some sound associated with the departure of the guard. He still thought that he must have a car somewhere in the vicinity. Then it occurred to him that most probably the guard had got back on the bus with the intention of handing the girl over to the authorities when they reached the frontier. There would certainly be a police post there of some importance, together with representatives of those whose job it was to deal with defectors and their like. He shivered at the thought. Would things now be different if he had given her the trust she had naïvely sought? Different for both of them?

However, this was no moment to reflect on what might have been. What he had to give his mind to was his own immediate future. Here he was lying in a ditch in a country which, he had every reason to suppose, regarded him with considerable unfriendliness. How was he going to get out?

After a couple of minutes hard thinking which brought him no nearer a solution of the core of his problem, he decided he must get as close to the frontier as he could under cover of darkness and possibly spend the whole of the next day lying up and observing. It might then be possible to work out an escape plan which he could put into operation the following night. Of course, if he were caught, no amount of talk was going to get him out of trouble. No country liked people who tried to slip in clandestine fashion across its borders, least of all the countries in that part of the world.

It was while he was morosely reflecting on the situation that he suddenly remembered that he still had his passport. He patted his jacket pocket. Yes, it was still there. He also had his wallet and that meant money. His spirits at once rose, but almost as soon sank again as he recalled German spies landed on the English coast during the war. They had passports and money and a good deal more besides, but it did not save most of them from a death on the prison gallows.

Well, this was not war and he was not a spy? Anyway, the first part was true, even though he might have trouble convincing the Bulgarian authorities of the second proposition.

But the possession of his passport was an undoubted advantage. It might yet be possible to cross the border openly.

A slight breeze had sprung up and he felt chilly. It was time to move. Moreover, nothing was worse for the morale than inaction.

He stood up and had walked a few steps along the ditch, when suddenly his foot struck something. He peered down but was unable to see the nature of the obstruction in the inky darkness which filled the ditch. Bending down, he put out a cautious hand and a second later started back as if he had touched a live wire.

What he most certainly had touched was a human leg!

With bumping heart, he cautiously set about investigating further.

The leg, he quickly discovered, was attached to a body which was covered over with a piece of tarpaulin. He stepped out of the ditch and crawled along to where the head was. By touch more than anything else, he concluded that it was the body of the girl whom the guard had removed from the bus. The girl who had called herself Paula Zwehl.

She was still warm, though he was unable to detect any sign of life. He felt his hands to see whether he had picked up any blood on them and was relieved to find that he had not. They were merely clammy with his own sweat.

He suddenly remembered her handbag and felt around for it in the ditch. He found it beneath her head which surprised him. It was too dark to examine it now, but he decided to take it with him. It might yet provide some clue to the ever growing list of mysterious and sinister happenings.

There was nothing he could do about the body except cover it over again. If it was Paula Zwehl, then Peacock's plan had fallen apart in achievement as well as in execution ... Beyond that it was futile to speculate, though thought of Peacock sent a spasm of fury through to his nerve ends. The more so as he pictured him at this moment at the port and cigar stage of a well served dinner.

With the handbag tucked firmly beneath his arm, he climbed out of the ditch and set off down the road.

During the first mile, he had to take cover only twice on account of cars passing, each coming from the direction of the frontier. Nevertheless he would halt every hundred yards or so and strain his eyes and ears for any danger signals.

It was gently undulating, open countryside with cultivated land stretching away on both sides of the road, which was intermittently lined with trees. The air was cool and sweet smelling, and high cloud obscured the stars.

Martin reckoned he had walked about five miles and must be within three or four of the frontier, when he decided to have a short rest. He looked at his watch and saw that it was just after half past eleven. It also occurred to him to wind it up. If he was going to be holed up for twenty-four hours or so, it was important to have an idea of time. A stopped watch could be irksome, if not disastrous.

As he sat with his feet resting in the ditch, he tried to imagine what his clerk and the other members of Chambers would say if they could see him now. It was an exercise which brought him a certain amount of wry amusement. The legal world of the Temple was about as far away as the moon at this moment.

Even John, the clerk, whose imperturbability and capacity to mask surprise were renowned among those who spent their lives practising these arts, must surely have registered some emotion if he could have seen his head of Chambers sitting in the dark in a Bulgarian ditch wondering how many crimes he was going to have to commit to get himself out of the country.

Happily, John was short on imagination, though Martin felt he could see a faint flicker of disapproval on the clerk's face if confronted by news of his arrest. Disapproval that anyone in Chambers could, so to speak, be caught without his bowler hat and rolled umbrella.

However, he had no intention of John being confronted by such a piece of news if he could possibly help it. And, in that, he was not motivated by any finer feelings for the susceptibilities of his clerk!

He stood up, had a stretch and set off again at a brisk pace. He had gone about a quarter of a mile when he was stopped in his tracks by the sound of voices ahead. Ducking into the ditch, he lay there and listened with all the intentness of a stalking animal of prey.

The next moment surprise bowled him over like an ocean breaker, for what he heard was an English male voice saying in a somewhat peevish tone: 'Damn you! Do you realise what you did, Rache, you poured the bloody tea slops into my shoes?'

'I thought you still had them on,' a female voice replied.

'Well, I didn't. And now they're full of tea leaves.'

'Sorry.' The voice sounded anything but.

'Tea leaves of all clammy things!'

'Oh, stop carrying on, Heck, and come back into the tent. I'm getting cold.'

After a while, the voices became muffled and Martin deduced that Heck must have done as bidden and closed the tent flap behind him.

He moved cautiously forward and the outline of a car suddenly loomed up a few yards ahead of him. It was parked on the verge and one push would have sent it slithering over into the ditch.

It did not take him long to discover that it was an incredibly ancient car, an Austin 10 of pre-war vintage.

He crept out of the ditch and was moving stealthily past the car when the female voice spoke again.

'I'm sure I hear someone outside, Heck.'

'Probably a dog.'

'You'd better go and see.'

'Why?'

'It may be someone trying to take the car.'

'They'll be lucky.'

'Go and see, Heck.'

'God, you're a pest tonight, Rache.'

'I'm nervous.'

'If you're nervous here, what are you going to be like when we get among the Arabs.'

'I like Arabs. I always got on well with Abdul at college.'

'Abdul was born in Cardiff and had never been out of the country.'

'I definitely heard someone move then, Heck,' the female voice said shrilly. 'You deaf or something?'

It was at this moment that Martin finally located the tent. It was about four yards beyond the car and on the farther side of the ditch, pitched in the lee of a bank which provided it with perfect shelter from the field side and effectively camouflaged it from anyone using the road.

He was standing near the front offside of the car when Heck unfastened the tent flap and wriggled out. A second later, the beam of a torch was flashed in his direction.

'Crikey, you're right, Rache, there is someone by the car.'

'It's all right, I'm English, too,' Martin said in a low, urgent tone.

'Who are you, mate? You broken down or something?'

Heck approached and, in the reflected glow from the torch, Martin saw a long-haired, bearded young man in a baggy sweater and a pair of jeans. His feet were bare.

'I'll explain,' Martin said, 'but let's get under cover. I'm not too keen on being seen.'

He stepped down into the ditch, moved towards the tent and sat down. Meanwhile, the girl had appeared; or rather, part of her had, her head and shoulders sticking out from one end of the tent. Apart from the absence of a beard, she resembled the young man as to the length of hair and sloppy sweater. Martin thought it reasonable to suppose she was also wearing jeans on that part of her which was out of sight.

'Who are you?' she asked in a tone full of curiosity.

'My name's Martin.'

'Martin something or something Martin?'

'Martin something.'

'Fair enough. I'm Rache and that over there's Heck. What can we do for you?'

'I'm not sure, but I'm in a bit of trouble.'

'Who isn't?'

Martin saw the distant lights of an approaching car and scuttled away down the ditch until it had passed.

'Sorry about that,' he said on his return, 'but . . .'

'You act like someone on the run,' Heck cut in.

'That's what I am in one sense.'

'Do you always carry a handbag?' Rache inquired with interest.

Martin had forgotten he still had it clutched under his arm. 'That's also something which needs a bit of explaining,' he said, with a faint laugh. 'May I ask where you're making for?'

'India,' Rache replied.

Martin's glance went automatically to the battered car squatting on the verge a few yards from them.

'In that?'

'If it wills. We'll get there somehow,' she added. 'Anyway

there's no hurry.' She paused and then said somewhat sharply, 'Do you believe in hurry?'

'Not for its own sake.'

'I should hope not. You can come to India with us if you want. Can't he, Heck?'

'Anyone can come anywhere with us,' Heck replied obligingly.

'All I want at the moment is to get out of Bulgaria,' Martin said a trifle wearily.

'What's the problem?' It was Heck who spoke. He had sat himself down in the ditch opposite Martin and had lit a cigarette.

'The police may try and prevent me leaving.'

'What've you done?' Rache asked.

'What's it matter what he's done?' Heck retorted, 'That's his business.'

'Sure it's his business. He doesn't need to tell us anything,' Rache agreed. 'Anyway, all police are ticks. They're just oppressors.'

'Might you be prepared to help me get out of the country?'

'Why not?' Heck said casually.

'Why not?' Martin echoed. 'First, because you don't know anything about me, next because it could be dangerous and after that because it could land you in trouble.'

Heck shrugged. 'You sound all right. What do you want us to do?'

Martin was silent for several seconds. That was it, he was not sure what he did want them to do. They had turned up in his life with such utter unexpectedness that he had not had time to work out a plan. Their apparent willingness to help him was touching, their lack of any sense of reality frightening. They were a couple of guileless children, international in outlook, yet unworldly in their casual approach to matters practical.

'I tell you what I think'll be best,' he said while they sat watching him. 'I'll go off and get a few hours sleep and return in the morning. What time were you proposing to leave?'

'When we're ready.'

'Six? Seven? Eight?'

'Depends when we wake.'

'As soon as it's light,' Rache broke in firmly. 'There's not going to be much sleeping done where you've pitched the tent tonight, Heck. It's like lying on the battlements.'

'O.K.,' Martin said, standing up. 'I'll go and find somewhere to doss down for a few hours and I'll be back around dawn. By then I'll have worked something out.'

He was about to move off into the darkness when he remembered something.

'Do you have a spare torch by any chance?' he asked.

'No, but you can have this one,' Heck replied.

'Aren't you going to need it?'

'I've got a lighter and there are some matches somewhere. You can take the torch.'

Martin accepted it with murmured thanks. Their attitude of complete trust was almost an embarrassment. He was not used to it in his own world of civilised and urbanely concealed selfishness.

The reason for which he wanted the torch was to examine the contents of the handbag. He hoped he might find something which would help him formulate a plan.

He walked along the ditch for about fifty yards and then struck across the field on his right in the direction of a small clump of bushes which he could see silhouetted against the less inky darkness of the sky.

With considerable caution he pushed his way into the clump which proved to be ring-shaped with a small cleared area in the middle. He sat down and opened the handbag, holding the torch right inside so that no light should escape. Before examining any of its contents, however, he focused his concentration on familiarising himself with the sounds of the area. These were mostly the rustling of leaves in his immediate vicinity, supplemented by an occasional animal cry of a hunter or its prey.

Pulling out her passport, he cradled it beneath his legs and used one hand as a cowl for the torch. With the other he turned the pages.

It had been issued by the East German authorities only three weeks before and was in the name of Paula Zwehl who was shown as having been born in Dresden on 11th February 1937. She apparently now lived in Berlin and her occupation was given as 'secretary'. But the page to which Martin gave most attention was that bearing Paula Zwehl's photograph. He stared at it for a long time, but even so was unable to decide whether it was the girl who had taken Anna Schmidt's place on the bus. Passport photographs were so notoriously bad that it might have been. On the other hand there was no certainty about it.

It was while he was still staring at it, that a thought struck him with the impact of a bucket of water poured over an unsuspecting head.

If the girl on the bus, and now lying in a ditch, really was Paula Zwehl—the Paula Zwehl who was the focal point of Peacock's elaborate plan—what on earth was she doing with an East German passport?

Quickly he turned the pages again, only to confirm his suspicions. There was no visa for Turkey and, even more definite, that country was not among those for which the passport had been validated. So how was she proposing to enter Turkey? And if she was not proposing to do so, what was she up to? There seemed to be only one answer to that. The girl calling herself Paula Zwehl was an imposter. He recalled how she and the guard had conversed in Bulgarian ... But why had she been left dead in the ditch, if, as now seemed likely, she was some sort of agent of that country? It was easy to believe that the real Paula Zwehl had been arrested—that would have followed Anna Schmidt's detention and the blowing apart of the whole rescue plan—but it still left an unexplained mystery of the fake Paula Zwehl. Unless ... unless the girl in the ditch *was* the real Paula Zwehl and was going to be slipped another passport at the right moment...

He put the passport on the ground at his side and turned his attention to the handbag's other contents.

A powder compact, a lipstick, a handkerchief with the initial 'P' woven at one corner, a purse containing Bulgarian and Turkish money. (That seemed to indicate an expected entry into Turkey.) And a small diary. Martin seized on this and eagerly began to turn its pages. It showed Paula Zwehl's name on the first, together with the same Berlin address as appeared in the passport. The remaining entries, however, were disappointingly few and seemed to relate to social fixtures. There were a number which read, 'Willi 7.30' or 'Willi 8' even 'Willi 11.30'. There was also a record of visits to concerts and the opera. 'Tristan' appeared against a date in March and 'Traviata' against one in April.

He flipped through the pages until he came to the present week. There was an entry of two days back which read 'Sofia an'. So this girl had arrived in Sofia only two days ago. After that, there was nothing else, save a brief entry which appeared to refer to return to Berlin in about ten days' time.

Martin put everything back into the handbag and closed it. Then he stood up and eased his chilled limbs. It should begin getting light around four o'clock, which gave him just over two hours to decide what to do. Sleep was out of the question. It was a long time since he had slept out in the open. It required practice and also his brain was in far too active a state to succumb to rest.

He set about reviewing the courses open to him. First, he had to decide whether to 'make use' of Heck and Rache or whether to rely on his own resourcefulness when he reached the border area. He realised that the decision was already made. If he did not throw his lot in with his new-found friends, he would have to spend the whole of the coming day in hiding and not attempt to get near the frontier until the next night. A loss of twenty-four hours, which was an unthinkable prospect; as well as one in which the possibility of danger grew by the hour.

So he would travel with Heck and Rache in their antiquated car. The next question was, should he do so openly or concealed? There did not seem to be much doubt about the answer to that. In the first place, there was nowhere in the car to hide anyone and in the second, even if there had been, the possibility of discovery by border guards was strong and then they would all end up in trouble. And the one thing he was determined not to do was involve them in any greater danger than that inherent in actually giving him a lift.

That was it, then. He would travel openly, armed with his own respectable British passport with its Bulgarian visa and its validation for all countries of the world. If he was going to be arrested, better to be in a position to fight back from a stance of legality, than to be caught trying to smuggle himself out like a hot piece of contraband.

Once you applied your mind to a decision, it was funny how often it presented itself as the only viable possibility.

He sat down again and then lay back in an endeavour to rest, if not to sleep. But the ground was hard and uneven and there seemed to be something approaching a minor gale at ground level. He stood up and decided to leave his cover and return to the ditch. Before doing so, however, he buried the handbag in loose earth beneath one of the bushes.

It was a few minutes after four o'clock when he crept back along the ditch to where Heck and Rache had spent the night. There was a moment of panic when he thought they might merely have existed in some fantasy dream and he would find the site as though they had never been. But no, there was the ancient car, and there a few yards farther on the small tent.

The sky to the east had begun to pale with the first grey light of dawn, when he called out softly, 'Are you awake in there?'

'Never more so,' Heck's voice answered. A second later, he emerged and stood up. 'God, how I hate this hour of the day,' he said busily scratching himself. 'Though it's said to be good for meditation. Rache says so, anyway.' He aimed a kick at the side of the tent. 'Wake up, woman, everyone's waiting.'

Rache clambered out yawning and then also set about having a good scratch.

'What are we waiting for?' she asked.

A couple of minutes later the tent had been stuffed into the car and a space of sorts had been made for Martin in the back. At first his head touched the roof, but then he removed the kettle on which he had negligently sat.

'What's for breakfast?' Heck asked as the car lurched forward on to the road.

'There are just three plums left,' Rache announced.

'Fine. Pass them round then.'

'I'm sorry I've got nothing to offer,' Martin said.

'Do you have any money?' Heck inquired.

'Yes.'

'We'll be able to stock up en route then. That is, if you're willing to spend it.'

'Very willing.' If given the chance, he wanted to add.

Heck let down his window and spat out his plum stone.

A signpost showed the frontier to be five kilometres away. The car's engine raced excitedly as if eager to be there.

CHAPTER EIGHT

The final stretch of road was dead straight. The Bulgarian frontier post straddled it like a filling station, the building surmounted by the huge red star, which the communist countries have appropriated as a symbol of the 'people's' vitality.

'If anything goes wrong and I'm detained,' Martin said, 'I'd be very grateful if you would inform the British Consul in Istanbul.'

'British consuls are almost as bad as the police,' Rache remarked. 'They just don't want to know one. Not the likes of us, anyway. Getting money out of them is harder than trying to borrow from your landlord.'

'I suppose it's because they're handling tax-payers' money,' Martin observed mildly.

'It doesn't worry them spending taxpayers' money on nuclear weapons,' she retorted scornfully.

The last thing Martin wanted at this of all moments was to get involved in the sort of political-cum-moral discussion he could see looming up.

'True,' he said pacifically. 'By the way I haven't told you my surname. It's Ainsworth.'

'I think names are degrading,' Rache said.

Martin decided to let this comment pass since they were now within fifty yards of the frontier post and a guard with a rifle slung over his shoulder was motioning them into one of the parking bays.

Heck braked to a halt under the suspicious eye of the guard, who walked round the car as though it were something just dredged up.

There appeared to be no one else about, though lights shone through one or two of the windows. A couple of large lorries and trailers were parked over on the far side and nearer the main building were three or four cars bearing Bulgarian plates. A quarter of a mile beyond lay the Turkish post which looked almost identical in the grey light of an early morning. Though instead of a red star, the country's national flag dominated the scene.

Never had Martin thought that he would have occasion to look upon the territory of a N.A.T.O. ally with such fervent longing.

The guard was pointing at a door, one of whose multilingual signs read 'Passport Control'.

Heck climbed out. 'Get moving, Rache, and bring your flipping passport this time.'

'Frontiers! Passports! God, will the world never learn!' Martin followed them across to the passport office, trying to give an impression of weary nonchalance.

Inside, a man was sitting at a table on the farther side of a counter. For several seconds he let them stand there while he went on reading the form which was spread out in front of him.

Rache made a disparaging face at him and scuffed her feet. Heck shrugged and began to whistle quietly. Martin just stood, counting seconds which seemed like hours.

After keeping them waiting for the best part of two minutes, the man rose, came over to the counter and, without a word, collected their passports and the car documents. He then disappeared through a door into another room.

'Bastard!' Rache said. 'This may be a people's democracy, but the police still behave like fascist pigs. Just because we're students and don't bow our heads before their petty nationalistic regulations, they treat us like mongrel dogs in an Arab slum.'

'Belt up, Rache,' Heck said. 'It's too early in the morning for vehemence. Try a bit of meditation instead.'

Rache stomped over to a bench seat and lay down full length on it, leaving Martin unsure whether this was a demonstration of dudgeon or an acceptance of Heck's advice.

It was about five minutes before the official reappeared. When he did so, it was to beckon to Martin to follow him back through the door.

Martin's heart performed a yo-yo manoeuvre.

'Don't keep us waiting too long,' Heck said lightly, with a flip of the hand, as Martin made his way round the end of the counter.

They were words in which, in some curious way, he took considerable comfort.

The room into which he followed the official was small and smelt strongly of stale cigar smoke.

'You speak German?' the official asked in that language, seating himself at a desk on which there were a mass of loose papers and two telephones. Behind him was a second door, which, Martin reckoned, must lead into another private room.

'Yes.'

'You're the Englishman, Ainsworth?'

'I'm English and my name is Ainsworth, yes.'

'You travel from England with these other two?'

That the man knew something about him was obvious. How much he knew remained to be seen. But at least Martin's own reaction to the questions was now determined.

'No, I met them last night for the first time. About seven kilometres back down the road if you really want to know.'

'That sounds very strange,' the man said in a sneering voice. 'Can you explain?'

'Very easily,' Martin said boldly. And you needn't think you're going to catch me out either, he thought. 'I was a passenger on a bus belonging to the German Company of Herold Touring A.G. I boarded the bus at Munich and was booked through to Istanbul.' As if you didn't know all this already, he reflected grimly. 'About ten o'clock last night, the bus stopped for a few minutes as one of the passengers wasn't feeling well. I got out, too, and the next thing I knew was the bus had gone off without me. I ran after it shouting, but nobody can have heard, so there I was left alone at the road-side. I hoped I might be able to thumb a lift and catch the bus here at the frontier. But the only two cars which came along didn't stop, so all I could do was to start walking. I had gone about four kilometres, when I came across this young couple who were camping beside their car and they very kindly offered to take me all the way to Istanbul. And when I get there I intend to have things out at the Herold Touring office. Leaving a passenger stranded like that was a disgraceful piece of carelessness.'

He had warmed to his story as he told it, as he had noticed the other's increasingly non-plussed expression. Obviously it had been hoped that he would launch into some concocted tale which they were in a position to refute. Whereas, there was every indication that he had said nothing in respect of which he could be tripped up.

He had been left to stand and he now glanced ostentatiously round for a chair on which to sit down. Unfortunately, the only one available was in a farther corner and he could only have reached it by climbing over the desk or by shifting his interrogator.

'A very curious story,' the man said. 'How do I know you're telling the truth?'

'Because it is the truth,' Martin replied, now feeling well on top. To a lawyer versed in the art of cross-examination, it was readily apparent that the man was fishing for information rather than testing a story of inherent weakness from a position of strength. It could only mean that the girl in the ditch had not yet been discovered. If the official found some pretext for detaining him, the tide could easily turn against him since it could not be very long before the body was discovered.

The man's next question confirmed the impression Martin

had already formed.

'There was a girl sitting next to you on the bus, yes?'

'Yes.'

'Where is she now?'

Martin appeared to look puzzled.

'Which girl are you referring to? There were two.'

'The second girl,' the man said stonily.

Martin thought rapidly. They must know that she had not been on the bus when it crossed the frontier. They would certainly have been looking out for her if she was one of their own agents. Somebody, at least, would have been tipped off about her presence on the bus and been told to facilitate whatever needed facilitating. Yes, that must be right, for if they had not known to expect her on the bus, they would not have missed her and the man facing Martin across the desk would not now be asking blind questions about her. Martin's dilemma was not knowing what explanation the bus crew had given for her absence. It must have been a satisfactory one or the bus would not have been allowed through. Or was it just possible that, for some reason, her non-presence on the bus had not been noticed at the time? In which case no explanation would have been called for and Martin could say what he liked without danger of incrimination.

The man was idly turning the pages of his passport, while all this was being swiftly computerised in Martin's mind. He suddenly had the feeling that the man's instructions had been to twist his tail a little and then allow him to go, unless, of course, he broke down and confessed to being an enemy of the people. If it had been otherwise, the interrogation would certainly not have been left in the hands of the official on duty. There would have been a high-powered team such as Borovets had provided.

But, *of course*, the girl's non-presence on the bus could not have been noticed at the time! If it had been, they would still be interrogating the passengers now. Assuming, that is, that she was a planted agent...

Pick your answer, Martin Ainsworth, and hope for the best.

'I've no idea where she is now,' he replied, as though surprised by the question. 'I imagine she is where the bus took her. Namely in Istanbul. I never saw her again after the bus went off without me.'

'You are saying that she left the bus later?'

'I'm saying that she was still on it when I saw its rear lights disappearing down the road.'

'She was not the passenger who became ill?'

'No, that was a Persian woman.'

The man's tone had become perfunctory and his interest in the interrogation seemed to have evaporated. He pushed back his chair and stood up. Picking up the three passports from the desk he led the way back into the other room. There he stamped the passports and handed Martin's back to him. Its comforting return made Martin feel like someone who wakes up in his own safe bed after a series of disturbing dreams.

He could see Heck and Rache standing over by the car and a Customs Officer peering in at the back. He was flooded with a sudden feeling of warm affection for his two new-found friends and their absurdly antiquated car, as he walked across to join them.

'Nice timing,' Heck said casually. 'This guy's just about finished his examination.'

'I'm hungry,' Rache announced, with a yawn.

'We should be able to buy some food at the Turkish post,' Martin said, wishing them there already.

He could hardly wait for them to be on their way. There was something strangely eerie about a frontier, especially one fortified with barbed wire and mines and guards who shot to kill. A sinister calm reigned until the moment when some poor human rabbit set off the whole lethal apparatus, and little chance he would then have.

As he gazed at the line of wire fence stretching away across the fields on each side of the road, he reflected on the utter hopelessness of his ever having been able to make an undetected crossing. He would have had to have worked his way south towards the barren, inhospitable-looking mountains which marked the frontier with Greece, and, even so, without any guarantee of success.

At last they were ready to go. Documents had been returned, the Customs and Passport Control officers had returned inside and the guard had raised the pole which barred the road. They drove past him and headed for the Turkish post a quarter of a mile ahead.

Martin let out the largest sigh of relief of his life. Even as he did so, however, he became aware of a car somewhere behind, feverishly flashing its headlights. He turned to look through the rear window and saw a small saloon come to a screeching halt outside the building they had just left. Two men jumped out and dashed inside.

Before anyone reappeared, Heck had braked the car to a halt.

'Turkey,' he announced. He gave the back of Rache's neck an affectionate squeeze. 'Get your passport out again, you infidel.'

There was greater evidence of activity on this side of the border than on the Bulgarian. Not only were there more offices and outbuildings, but also many more officials about, including a fair number of soldiers in uniform. One of these, a lad of not more than twenty, was staring at the car with undisguised fascination.

Martin was watching him when he saw him turn his head abruptly as one of his companions shouted something. He followed the line of their gaze which was along the stretch of road joining the two posts.

Standing in the middle of the road just in front of the barrier at the Bulgarian end were two men. Each of them was holding a pair of heavy binoculars to his eyes and it was not difficult to surmise the object of their study. It could only be the ancient Austin and its three passengers.

Clearly, 'Paula Zwehl's' body had been discovered.

CHAPTER NINE

The Turkish officials were thorough, but uncommunicative, in the discharge of their duties. They seemed to view Martin and his companions without enthusiasm, and released them on their way about half an hour later with an air of formal despatch.

'I can't wait to get to a country where money isn't everything,' Rache commented, as the car crested a slope and left the frontier out of sight behind. 'Once they see you haven't got any money to spend in their countries, they treat you like vermin. It makes you sick.'

'I doubt whether you'll find it any different between here and India,' Martin remarked, 'indeed, the poorer the country, the more interested it is in its visitors' pounds and dollars and francs.'

'There's no hope for the world until we do away with all the narrow monetary systems which throttle the ordinary people's aspirations.'

'Stop politicking,' Heck said. 'Imperialists, communists, capitalists, they're all as bad as one another when you get to governmental level.'

'What do you advocate?' Martin asked.

'I? I don't advocate anything. I'm not trying to put the world straight—at least not until I've got myself straight. And whether I ever manage that remains to be seen. Probably not. All I ask, meanwhile, is to be left in peace to discover myself. Who I am and why I am.'

'You're too naïve, Heck,' Rache remarked.

'Better that than to be a sophisticated smart-alec.'

'I'm famished,' Rache said, with her knack for abrupt changes of subject. 'How far is the nearest town? It was bloody rotten not being able to buy anything back at the frontier. They ought to keep those shops open round the clock.'

'Just for you, I suppose. Never mind the poor sods who have to be on duty.'

'Stop nagging, Heck, there's a love! You still haven't said how far it is to a town?'

'We should reach Edirne in just under half an hour by my reckoning,' Martin said. 'We'll definitely be able to buy some food of sorts there.'

The road along which they were travelling ran straight in a long continuing switchback as it cut across a gently undulating landscape which was remarkable for its bareness of trees. There were occasional villages to left or right, consisting of a few white-washed one-storey houses with the inevitable mosque, its minaret resembling a slender missile of a newer age.

It was a quarter to seven when they reached Edirne and its narrow streets were already full of people. Heck pulled up outside a row of dilapidated shops, which gave an impression of swarming activity.

'I suggest you and Rache go shopping and I'll mind the car,' Martin said, handing over forty Turkish lire.

'What's this worth?'

'Between twenty-five and thirty bob.'

'We'll be able to buy up the whole place.'

'I doubt it. If I know anything, the prices are going up even as we talk.'

'They haven't met Rache. She was born in a bazaar.'

Martin watched them disappear inside what looked like a general store on the other side of the road.

During the twenty minutes or so that they were gone, he was made to feel like a fish in a tank as countless faces came and peered at him through the car window. Most of them, too, were not content merely to peer, but were eager to sell him something or to beg money from him. Two small urchins wished to clean his shoes and when he rejected this offer, one of them produced a pair of scissors and appeared to propose he should succumb to a haircut.

It was with a fair measure of relief that he saw Heck and Rache returning, each hugging a huge brown paper bag. He had not only begun to feel hungry himself, but to experience a build-up of tension as a result of sitting in the car and being stared and mouthed at. His skin felt tacky and he knew he must look as dirty as some of the children who had been gazing at him with animated interest.

'I hope you don't mind,' Heck said, 'but we spent all your money.'

'He intended us to,' Rache put in. 'Didn't you, Martin?'

'Sure. What have you bought?'

'Apricots, some heavenly honey things, bread, goat's milk, eggs the size of hailstones and some odd-looking meat which smells as if it's been marinated in the drains. And some cheese, too.'

A few miles out of Edirne, they stopped and had their breakfast at the roadside. The sun had gathered warmth and the scene was as pleasant and peaceful as one could have wished.

Heck and Rache, whose nature it was to take each day as it came, seemed untroubled by anything that had happened, least of all by Martin's malignant invasion of their lives. He was immensely grateful for and touched by their incurious acceptance of him. It would be nice to think that no harm could befall such trusting innocents, but he was only too well aware of the existence of danger. Where and in what shape it would strike he did not know, but those men with their binoculars had not just been casual observers of a scene down the road. They had been professional hunters who were used to seeking their quarry with relentless determination. They were not the sort to be put off by a temporary thwarting.

Martin chewed tentatively at a piece of the meat which tasted rather as it smelt, while Heck and Rache tucked in with voracious intensity. No one spoke.

The road was busy with traffic. Enormous, heavy commercial lorries with trailers, ramshackle buses bulging with passengers and private cars, most of whose occupants gave the appearance of being officials of one sort or another. Indeed, a fair number of them actually were in uniform.

'I feel better,' Rache said, leaning back contentedly. 'I've not eaten so well since we left home.'

'She's forgotten she only used to live on cups of coffee back in London.'

'And slices of pizza.'

'When there was any over.' Heck turned to Martin. 'We used to take most of our meals at a small espresso bar owned by an Italian called Guido. We usedn't to go there till after midnight and Guido would often let us have left-overs for free or at least for sixpence or so.'

'What were you doing in London before you set out on this trip?' Martin asked.

'What were we doing, Rache?' Heck repeated in a wry tone.

'You wouldn't believe it to look at him,' Rache said 'but Heck has a degree in Sociology, once worked in an advertising agency...'

'For eight weeks.'

'As a clerk in the Ministry of Overseas Development...'

'For six weeks. God, that was a bureaucratic white elephant of a department.'

'And as a packer in a bookstore.'

'For four weeks only. That was the best job of the lot, but I got the push because I used to spend too much time reading the books and not enough packing them. People wrote in complaining that their books hadn't arrived. Three people to be exact. It was just that I had put their books on one side to read at more leisure.'

'That's the greedy, grubbing commercial world for you!' Rache commented with asperity. 'The sooner they get machines on to their dreary jobs, the better.'

'It wasn't a dreary job at all,' Heck protested. 'It was the most interesting of the lot.'

'It was dreary the way they wanted it done.'

'Perhaps. But you can't blame them. Not that I blame myself either!'

'Precisely, it's the rotten system!'

'Here we go again!' he taunted her.

She grinned. 'Your trouble is that you lack any fire in your belly.' Her grin broadened. 'All you have is tealeaves in your shoes.'

She spoke with such infectious good humour that Martin let out a cheerful laugh and Heck gave her a mock long-suffering smile.

Addressing Martin, he said, 'You wouldn't need three guesses, would you, to say where she was educated.'

'London School of Economics?'

'Right first time.'

'I only lasted a year there, though,' Rache added with a note of defiance.

'What happened then?'

'I couldn't be bothered to sit my exams. I just walked out. Anyway, I had an excuse.' Her expression clouded over. 'I was pregnant. It wasn't Heck's and it's been adopted and it's got a far better mum than I'd have ever been to it.' She paused. 'But don't think that having a baby doesn't do something to you! A bit of me has gone with it for ever.'

There was a silence, and then Heck jumped up.

'Shall we go?'

'Why don't we sit here a bit longer?' Rache said. 'It's nice and peaceful. And anyway, who's in a hurry?'

Heck sat down again.

'There's something we ought to talk about,' Martin said, 'and that's me. I'm worried that I'm going to make trouble for you by sticking around. I can never thank you sufficiently for what you've done for me, but I'm afraid I'm definitely an albatross round your necks and I would never forgive myself if I were the cause of your landing in serious trouble.'

'What sort of trouble?' Heck inquired.

'I don't know, but I suppose you could find yourselves held by the police on some pretext or other, and this is not a part of the world where habeas corpus applies.'

'I take it you're some sort of agent?' Heck said.

'If the countries of the world used all the money they spend on spying to alleviate hunger and suffering,' Rache broke in, 'it'd be a happier place for everyone.'

'I wholeheartedly agree,' Martin said to her obvious surprise. 'I am not a spy in the true sense,' he continued. 'On the other hand I was involved in a minor way in helping to get someone out of Bulgaria illegally. The plan went hopelessly wrong and the result was I became a man on the run.'

'But they let you out all right,' Rache said.

'That was because they didn't have an excuse to hold me.'

'But now it's different, is that what you're saying?' Heck asked.

'Yes, Did you notice a car dash up to the Bulgarian side of the border just as we reached the Turkish?'

'I saw some men with binoculars.'

'Those binoculars were trained very firmly on us,' Martin said.

'So?'

'I don't think my departure from Bulgaria is the end of my difficulties. And my difficulties will rub off on you so long as I remain in your company.'

'What is it the Bulgarians know now which they didn't know before you left their country? Or am I not meant to ask questions of that sort?'

'No, I've not got anything to hide. I'm just trying to extricate myself from the stinking mess of betrayal and doublecrossing, which I've been caught up in. As to the first part of your question, I reckon that the Bulgarians have now found the body of a girl in a ditch not very far from where I met you.'

'Who killed her?' Rache asked sharply.

'I didn't, but I don't know for sure who did. In fact, I don't know at all. I don't even know who the girl is. I . . . well, I told you, the whole thing is a hopeless, bewildering, dangerous mess.'

'What do you expect they'll do?'

'I don't even know *that*. What to expect, I mean. But they'll have the particulars and description of the car and it's not a very difficult one to spot, so they may well try and stop it before we reach Istanbul. I've looked at a map and this is the only road leading to the city from the west, so it would be quite easy for them to get on our tail. Beyond that I just don't know.' He shrugged helplessly. 'The only thing for certain is that I've become an object of unwelcome interest to what might be called hostile forces.'

'What do you suggest?'

'If you're prepared to go on taking the risk, I'd like to ride with you to within a reasonable distance of Istanbul and then make my own way into the city. I think that way, too, there'll be less risk of anything disagreeable happening to you. If you are stopped on reaching the city you can deny knowing anything about me or my whereabouts. You can just tell anyone who asks that you gave me a lift after I'd said how I'd been left behind by the bus on which I was travelling. Incidentally, it was a Herold Touring bus in case you're cross-examined ... It's possible nothing'll happen at all ... On the other hand, enough has already happened to make it more probable that something will. Something directed against me, that is.'

'Do you mean somebody may actually try and kill you?' Rache asked in an outraged tone.

'No I don't think that, but I think they—whoever *they* are— believe I know something about *what's* happened, when in fact I don't.'

'I don't pretend to understand a thing about it. It all sounds like a spy script before the plot's been properly worked out, but as far as I'm concerned, you're welcome to continue the journey.'

'That goes for me, too,' Heck said, stretching. 'I suppose we might as well get going, now that that's settled.'

Martin felt a lump in his throat—a lump of true gratitude for their unselfish willingness to help him. Though they had, on this occasion, actually asked a few questions on what he had told them, he was still astonished by their trusting acceptance of his company and their unconcerned attitude towards the risks it entailed. They were indeed true to their own simple creed of living.

He rose and, before getting back in the car, gazed in each direction along the road which snaked across the undulating landscape. He had already begun to chafe at its exasperating monotony. Each time a ridge was crested, it was in the hope that something different would be revealed on the farther side. But always it was the same, another dip, another ridge a mile or more on, and the road disappearing tantalisingly over the rim.

Heck pushed the car along at a steady 40 m.p.h., driving bent forward over the wheel as though to urge it on. Rache sat beside him with one arm rested along the back of his seat. Martin had asked her if she drove and she had replied that she did not, which had caused him to reflect that Heck's spine was going to be irreparably bent by the time they reached India. Except that the prospect of the car ever completing the journey seemed wildly remote. On the other hand, he would never have believed it would have got so far as it had without the evidence of his own senses. It was not the sort of car he would, in normal circumstances, have trusted himself to ride in from Hyde Park Corner to Marble Arch.

Sitting squashed in the back, he kept an alert eye open for any sign of danger. He constantly looked out of the rear window to see if they were being followed and gave particular attention to any parked cars they passed. On one occasion, such a car did pull off the verge as soon as they had gone by to remain a steady hundred yards behind them for the next two or three miles. At Martin's request, Heck reduced speed and the car overtook them, a couple of cheerful youths grinning and waving as it did so.

Around the middle of the morning, Rache suddenly let out an excited cry.

'Look! Sea!'

She pointed over to the right where a stretch of water had just come into view.

'That must be the Sea of Marmara,' Martin said.

'Let's go and have a swim,' she said.

'Good idea,' Heck replied. 'When we get a bit closer, I'll turn off and we'll find a lonely stretch with a bit of luck, where we can go in as nature made us.'

Martin reckoned that they were now about twenty miles from Istanbul. Already there were the beginnings of urbanisation, small haphazard outcrops of dwellings and straggling villages which were obviously satellites.

A few miles farther on, Heck turned off the main highway and they bounced and rattled along a track leading in the direction of the sea, which they reached with unexpected suddenness. The track cut through a dune, did a right angle turn to the left and there it was, small, lazy waves breaking on a loose sandy beach.

Heck stopped the car and they all got out. From there the track ran parallel with the water to what looked like a half completed hotel a mile farther on. But there was no sign of anyone about.

In less than a minute, Heck and Rache had stripped off their clothes and were dashing into the sea.

'I hope to God no one sees them,' Martin murmured to himself. It would be ironic if, after all his warnings of danger, they got themselves arrested for offending Turkish susceptibilities in regard to naked bathers.

For a time he stood watching them as they splashed around like a couple of kids. Then he wandered off and sat down in a hollow between two dunes.

The sand was soft and the sun deliciously warm. He lay back, his hands clasped behind his head, and sleep crept up on him with irresistible stealth.

He awoke with a start and at first thought he must have slept for several hours, but a glance at his watch revealed that only forty minutes had passed.

He was about to stand up when he heard voices coming from the direction of the car. He was unable to distinguish what was being said, but it was immediately apparent that it was not just Heck and Rache conversing.

Cautiously he got to his feet and moved to where he could see and hear what was happening.

Heck and Rache were standing fully dressed with their backs against the car and facing them were the two cheerful youths who had overtaken them on the road earlier in the morning.

The only difference was that now there was nothing cheerful about them. One of them was holding a revolver which was pointed at Heck's stomach and the other had a vicious-looking knife in his hand. Their expressions were hard and scowling.

As Martin stood watching in horror, the one with the gun said, 'Where? Where man? Quick tell or ...' The sentence was completed by a meaningful thrust of the weapon in his hand.

'I've told you, I don't know where he is. He's gone ... disappeared.'

The one with the knife suddenly seized Rache's wrist with his other hand.

'Quick, you tell where.'

Rache screamed as the blade of the knife was drawn pitilessly across his forearm.

'Tell or I make more cuts,' the youth snarled.

Martin gave a shout and dashed forward.

'Stop that, you little bastard!'

The two thugs turned in his direction, a look of malicious satisfaction spreading over both their faces. The one with the gun stepped forward pointing it at his middle, but Martin was too full of cold fury to pay them any heed. He went up to Rache who was gripping her wounded arm with her other hand and gazing at the seeping blood with a stunned expression.

Heck, too, seemed to have been shocked into immobility. But suddenly he shook himself and taking hold of her arm sucked at the wound.

'It's all right, love,' he said, 'it's not deep. If we can find a clean bit of something, I'll cover it over.'

Martin stood there at a loss for words. He had put an arm round Rache's shoulder, but found nothing to say. Nothing which would not sound trite and banal.

Finally he said, 'I'll get out of your way now. I'm bitterly sorry to have brought all this on you and I can't thank you enough.'

The youth with the revolver came up and jabbed it into Martin's side.

'Come,' he said angrily.

Martin turned and began walking along the track, his captors keeping a pace behind him.

They had gone about ten yards when he heard one of them running back. He looked round and saw the one with the knife slashing the tyres of Heck's car.

He felt sick and wretched as he never had before. To have been the cause of such cruel spite being vented on others was almost more than he could bear. He was beyond caring what happened to himself, though at the back of his mind he knew that it was only a matter of time before his determination to survive reasserted itself.

But at this particular moment, he would have done nothing to save himself if his thuggish captors had taken him behind a sand dune for summary execution.

Perhaps, he told himself, he only felt that way because he knew that would not happen.

These were hired kidnappers, not executioners. Shortly, he would know who had hired them: who it was who considered him to be worth such swift and ruthless seizure—and why.

CHAPTER TEN

There were some days when Peacock felt that his superiors were quite unaware of the strains imposed upon him by his work. They took for granted his long hours—he seldom left the office before seven o'clock each evening—and the not infrequent Saturdays and Sundays when duty would require him to be back at his desk.

The upper reaches of the government service were geared to this sort of routine, to sudden crises blowing up at week-ends, though admittedly it was not as bad nowadays as it had been in the thirties when Hitler used, it seemed, to put Saturdays aside for drilling on Europe's sensitive nerve spots. But it was still bad enough and at times it even got down such an urbane and sardonic servant as Peacock.

The past week had been a particularly trying one with practically everything going wrong save his carefully mounted Balkan operation. It seemed that Ainsworth had been the right choice for that minor rôle and that at least was a relief. You never knew in advance with the non-pros, however. When they were good, they were very, very good, and when they were bad, they were disastrous.

And thinking of Ainsworth, there should be something further through from Hart very shortly. By now the operation must have been successfully concluded and Hart should, indeed, have reported already.

Peacock sighed heavily. It was a capricious providence that made even the best of his field managers defective in some aspect of their work. Brian Hart was the Lawrence figure of the service. But damn him for not keeping his superiors informed all the time.

Good news was just what Peacock needed at the moment. Not that it would be the sort of news which could be breezed around, or even the sort which was of interest to his political bosses. Indeed, it was the sort of operation which it was better they should know nothing about. It made them jumpy and they were never really persuaded of the necessity to spend a great deal of money and even more time in effecting the rescue of a single, anonymous agent.

Since they spent a great deal of their own time writing off commitments running into hundreds of millions of pounds and making, and then reversing, decisions to the prejudice of millions of their fellow creatures, such an attitude was hardly surprising.

But it was not to please his political masters that Peacock wanted good news. It was to raise his own bruised morale and to know that he had not lost his touch in the successful planning of such an operation.

It was at times such as these when he wearied of the shadows in which his work took place, when he longed to answer back the criticism of some botched operation, concerning which the public had been told by a noisy press about one tenth, and that an inaccurate tenth. But the feeling never lasted long and, moreover, was never apparent to any of his staff.

'Have you finished?' his secretary asked, coming into his room. On days such as these, he lunched at his desk. One of the messengers would go to a nearby café and bring him back a carton of milk and some smoked salmon sandwiches, which his secretary would put on a tin tray which bore a somewhat stained picture of Big Ben and the Houses of Parliament.

'Yes, I have. Anything through from Munich yet?' he asked, as she picked up the tray.

'There's something just come in, I think. I'll go down and fetch it if it's urgent.'

'Please.'

A few minutes later, she came back into his room carrying the message. Something in her expression warned him to be ready for disagreeable news. He took the piece of paper from her.

It read:

'Complications. Ainsworth stampeding like rogue elephant and now in great personal danger. Suggest I fly Istanbul immediately to retrieve situation. Main operation successfully completed.'

CHAPTER ELEVEN

The car into which Martin was thrust was a small and ancient Mercedes. The springs of the back seat had long since given up any notion of teamwork and the floor was a mess of oily rags, old newspapers and empty cigarette packets. The vehicle was parked just where the track turned inland.

The youth with the revolver got into the back with Martin and the other took the driver's seat, carefully laying his knife at his side.

As they started to bump their way back towards the main road, and as Martin's initial shock began to wear off, he covertly studied his two captors.

Each was in his early twenties, the car driver possibly being

99

the older by a year or so. They appeared to be equals in the sense that neither gave the impression of being the boss.

The driver was swarthy, had a moustache and a mass of well-greased black hair which rose from his forehead like a tidal wave.

The one sitting at Martin's side was the tougher looking of the two. He was sallow, with brown melancholy eyes, a thin mouth and nostrils which resembled two dark round tunnels. He also had a well-covered head of greased black hair. He sat with the revolver resting on his knee, but pointing always in Martin's direction.

It was apparent from their demeanour that they were extremely pleased with the outcome of their morning's activity. They conversed animatedly and frequently laughed, and Martin was disagreeably reminded of two young hunters returning to camp after a particularly rewarding kill.

Just before they reached the main road, the driver looked at his watch and said something to his companion who made some noisy sounds with his mouth while he appeared to be thinking before venturing a reply.

They turned right in the direction of Istanbul and Martin sat up straighter to take better note of his surroundings. It was about the only positive course open to him. Escape was obviously out. He would be either shot dead or wounded before he was half out of the car. An opportunity might offer itself later, but not, he reckoned, so long as he remained in the custody of the present two. To them, he was far too valuable a prize to run risks with. Moreover, he thought it probable that they were mercenaries who were due to be paid· by results. And the result demanding full payment must surely be the handing over of himself in one piece to the hirer. No, all he could do for the present was to observe exactly where they were taking him and to take very special note of where they eventually stopped. Everything might depend on the accuracy of his observation of their final destination.

Suddenly to his surprise, the car turned off down a track to the left and headed in a cloud of dust towards a farm about half a mile away. The farm was on a slight ridge and the track dipped out of sight beyond it.

They did not stop at the farm, however, and drove on towards some dilapidated looking outbuildings in the hollow which lay farther on.

The car slowed down as it approached these buildings and the driver then swung it on to the patch of rough ground between two of them. He cut the engine and waited for the dust to subside. When it had done so, he jumped out, came round to Martin's side of the car and, opening the door, motioned him to get out. The youth with the revolver gave him a gentle jab in the ribs to make their wishes clearer.

The buildings, which looked unused and were in extremely derelict condition, might once have served for storage purposes. At one end, standing on its own, was what resembled a glorified pig-sty. Glorified only in the sense that it was made of stone and had a roof. Its solid wooden door was padlocked.

The driver pulled a key from his pocket, unlocked the door and flung it open. At the same moment, the other youth who was just behind Martin gave him a sharp push in the small of the back which propelled him inside.

The door was immediately shut and repadlocked. For a full minute, he stood still waiting for his eyes to become accustomed to the dark. Happily, it was not all that dark since there were wide cracks all round the door which let in a certain amount of light. The floor was uneven and consisted of beaten earth. A quick examination showed his cell to be quite bare. It was no more than a space enclosed by walls, roof and ground.

He stepped over to the door and put his eye against one of the cracks. The two youths were standing a couple of yards away smoking. He looked at his watch and saw that the time was one o'clock. He felt that he had lived three lives during the past twenty-four hours.

Reviewing his new situation, he decided that either this was the handing-over rendezvous or he was going to be kept here until after dark when they would continue their journey into the city. Of the two, he thought the second the more likely. But either way, he might as well try and get some rest. Happily, hunger had been more than satisfied by their roadside breakfast. Thoughts of this reminded him sharply of Heck and Rache, from whom he had parted less than an hour ago, but who now seemed to belong to another epoch. Standing in the centre of his tiny, darkened prison, he found himself offering up a quiet prayer for their safe preservation and welfare.

Later after a further look outside—the youth with the revolver was alone sitting on a stool facing the door—he stretched out on the ground and tried to force himself into sleep. Just when he was beginning to think it was hopeless, he drifted dreamlessly away.

He was awakened by bright sunlight on his face. The door was open and one of the youths was standing in the entrance staring down at him.

Martin felt chilled and stiff and yet, with it, refreshed. He looked at his watch and saw that he had been asleep three hours. Under the youth's watchful gaze, he rewound his watch and then sat up, hugging his knees.

The youth seemed relieved and Martin wondered whether he had thought that he might have died.

'Hungry?' the youth asked, pointing at his mouth.

'Thirsty,' Martin replied, going through the motions of drinking.

The youth nodded and, turning, called out something to his companion who was out of sight. A second or two later the other youth appeared carrying a tin mug, which he handed to Martin.

It was half full of very sweet, very thick Turkish coffee. Not exactly thirst quenching stuff, Martin decided, but it had the effect of bringing him further to life.

His two guards stood talking in the doorway while he drank it. When he had finished he got up and walked over to them, as if to step outside and take the air. But immediately the one with the revolver produced it from nowhere and pointed it at him while the other pushed him violently back inside.

'Not good. You stay,' said the knife-holding one.

'How long are we staying here?' Martin asked. He decided it was time to show a bit of spirit.

'Stay.'

'I know, so you've said, but for how long?'

'You see.'

'Where are we going from here?'

'Later.'

'I said *where*? Not *when*?'

'You see.'

'We're obviously going into Istanbul, so why can't you say so?'

'Too much talk. Not good.'

'You realise, I suppose, that you'll both end up in prison when this little lark is over?'

They obviously did not understand this, though the word 'prison' seemed to register. They frowned and exchanged a few words.

'Kidnapping a foreigner is a very serious offence under anyone's law,' Martin went on. 'And then there'll be a charge of
wounding and another of malicious damage or whatever the
Turkish equivalent is. It'll all add up to quite a few years in
prison for both of you.'

The fact that they clearly could not follow what he was
saying did not worry him. The object of the exercise was to
shake their confidence by expressing his own by tone of voice
and calm demeanour. He realised, however, that it was in fact
beyond his powers to shake their confidence sufficiently to
make any difference to the immediate outcome. Nevertheless,
he was aiding his own morale by treating them as a couple of
delinquents whom the law would catch up with in due course.

He was rewarded when they glared at him angrily and then
slammed the door shut. He went over to peer through one of
the cracks and see where they went. After speaking together
for a short time, the one with the knife sat down on the stool
and the other strolled out of sight. Probably to sit in the car,
Martin thought.

As he watched, his guard appeared to be thoughtfully sizing
up the door of his prison, then there was an incredibly quick
movement of his wrist, a hissing sound and a menacing thud as
the knife bedded itself in the wood.

It all happened so swiftly that Martin only jumped back
after it was over.

The youth retrieved his knife and returned to the stool
where he used it to clean his nails.

Martin sat down in the corner farthest from the door and
for the umpteenth time reviewed his situation. Events had
moved with such rapidity, that he had the impression of having lived four utterly separate lives in concertinaed continuity.

Three days ago—it seemed like three hundred years—he
had been a staid London barrister. A few hours later he was
playing a sort of James Bond rôle in a very minor key. Then
something had gone nightmarishly wrong and he had become
a victim of hostile interrogation and a fugitive in quick succession. And now finally he was a captive pawn in a game in
which he suspected the stakes to be frighteningly high. Each of
these metamorphoses seemed to have occupied a full lifetime
and it was reality itself which was dressed as fantasy. Not if he
had been whirling through space could he have experienced
greater disorientation, in the sense of nothing being related to
anything else. Each phase was separate and self-contained. At

the moment, his world consisted only of what he could see and hear in the darkened shed. Even Heck and Rache seemed to belong to a bygone life.

And, yet, he must try and orientate his thoughts, must see the events of the past three days in a continuing context, must draw some conclusions from what had happened. Not that that was very difficult! Peacock's plan had gone disastrously wrong and those involved in it were like torpedoed sailors. Some had drowned immediately, others drifted helplessly, clutching at pieces of floating wreckage in the lonely wastes of a friendless ocean.

Martin Ainsworth was one of these.

As the afternoon wore on, the shed became uncomfortably hot and its atmosphere, never fresh, positively fetid. From the position of the sun, it was not difficult to work out that the door faced almost due west, though this was not a particularly helpful piece of data.

Martin sat in his corner and watched the narrow shaft of light, which cleaved the edge of the door, become more elongated as the sun fell lower in the sky. An hour later the sun had set and he was sitting in complete darkness when the door was opened and one of the youths flashed a torch on him.

'Come,' he said.

Martin rose, brushed himself down in an automatic gesture, and stepped outside. They were both there, and each quickly ensured his awareness that they were still armed. They escorted him over to the car and he was motioned into the same seat as before. They too assumed their previous positions.

The car returned the way it had come and turned left on reaching the main road. They had been going for about a quarter of an hour when they reached the brow of a ridge and there stretching away in folds of light was Istanbul.

Martin instinctively leant forward to see better, but a prod in the ribs reminded him of the presence of his armed guard and he sat back again.

The new growth of city on the western flank seemed to go on endlessly and several times he thought they must be nearing the centre, only to realise they were still running through outer suburbs.

The road continued to switchback so that one minute there was a breathtaking view of twinkling lights as far as the eye could see: the next they were in a trough with a hotch-potch of old and new, but mostly new, buildings on either side and visibility limited to the next bus stop.

It was a wide, well-lit road and the driver seemed to increase speed the deeper they penetrated the built-up area.

They turned left at some traffic lights, tangled with a conglomeration of cars and buses in a large square and then shot away down an underpass.

Martin blinked. He had just caught sight of a large mosque when they were into the tunnel. He had not thought of Istanbul in terms of having such functional traffic refinements.

A few minutes later they had reached water level and were being funnelled towards the Galata Bridge. He was thankful that he had idly studied a plan of the city before leaving home. He knew that they were about to cross the Golden Horn to the part of the city known as Beyoglu and that beyond lay the Bosporus and on its far side Üsküdar, the Asiatic quarter of Istanbul. He had always had the happy facility of being able to carry maps and plans in his mind's eye and his bump of locality seldom deserted him.

His recollection was that the Galata Bridge crossed the Golden Horn almost where it joined the Bosporus and where the channel then opened out into the Sea of Marmara.

Half-way across the bridge, they were held up in traffic and the revolver was pressed meaningfully into his side to discourage any thought of escape he might be having. He pretended not to notice and continued to gaze out at the shimmering water and the host of craft which was plying up and down, as well as lining both sides. Motor launches, tugs, bloated ferries and old-fashioned freighters filled the scene like species of wild life on an African lakeshore.

The traffic eased and they moved forward again. On the farther side of the bridge, they left the main stream of cars and hurtled up a steep, narrow, ill-lit road which wound its way between anonymous-looking buildings. Before they reached the top, they turned left, then right, then left again, so that Martin had the impression that the driver was making the route deliberately difficult to follow. They cut across a main road and once more criss-crossed their way through a poorer district.

With a final lurch, the car turned down another narrow, potholed road and came to rest outside a pair of high wooden gates. The driver got out and ran across to bang on them.

There was no one in sight ahead and Martin turned to look out of the rear window. But the street appeared to be deserted.

Before he had time to take further stock of the situation, the gates were opened and they had driven into a small walled courtyard. The gates were immediately closed and bolted behind them by an elderly man with a brown leathery face and grizzled close-cropped hair, who then came and said something to the driver.

It is generally futile to try and divine the tenor of a conversation in an unknown language, but Martin gained the impression that these were not exactly words of welcome. The driver said something back in what sounded like an annoyed tone and the old man just shrugged. At that moment, a door in the side of the building opened and another man came out. He was about forty and tough-looking with Slavic features. But most apparent was his expression of boiling fury. The old man backed away and the new arrival let out a torrent of angry abuse at Martin's two captors. On this occasion, there could be no mistaking his meaning. He was flaying them and their expressions of sullen anger only went to confirm this.

When his flow of words ceased, the driver made what sounded like a resentful retort, which had the effect of releasing a further tirade at him and at his companion, who continued to hold the revolver pressed into Martin's side.

It was infuriating not to understand what was being said and not to know what the two young thugs had done to earn such a verbal lashing. By now the expressions on both their faces were sullen, tinged with spite.

When the man finished speaking the second time, there was a silence. He seemed to wait a few seconds to see whether all opposition had been subdued. Satisfied that it had, he came round to Martin's side of the car and opened the door. He, too, was now holding a gun in his hand.

He motioned Martin to get out and walk across to the door through which he had entered the yard. Without a further word to, or glance at, the thugs, he followed. Closing and locking the door behind them, he gestured with the gun to indicate that Martin was to walk along the passage ahead. It was stone-paved and had white-washed walls and was lit by a single low-powered naked bulb. There were no doors on either side, but fifteen yards along it made a right-angle turn. Immediately round the corner was a stone staircase. One flight led upwards, the other downwards.

Martin paused and the man nodded at the descending flight. At the bottom there was another shorter corridor with a door half-way along it on the right. The man opened the door and pushed Martin inside. The next thing he knew, the door had been slammed and locked and he could hear the man's retiring footsteps back along the corridor and up the stairs.

Martin gazed slowly around him, grateful that at least there was light whereby to do so. It was a single light fixed high up on one wall and covered over by a metal cage. There appeared to be no operating switch and so presumably the light was controlled from outside.

The room was about twelve feet by ten with white-washed walls and a stone floor. It had a high ceiling and a small heavily barred window well out of reach. In its simple way, it gave the impression of having been recently redecorated. At all events, it was surprisingly clean, almost aseptically so.

Along one wall was a low bunk-type bed with a blanket folded at one end. Apart from that the room contained no furniture whatsoever.

One thing stood out a mile: whatever the room had been originally, it had been deliberately adapted for use as a prison cell.

Martin looked at his watch and automatically rewound it as he did so. It was half past nine. He then stood concentrating his aural senses as intently as he could, but there was not a sound to be heard anywhere.

He was virtually entombed.

Because there was nothing else to do he lay down on the bed and gazed at the ceiling.

He must have been doing so for about half an hour when he heard footsteps approaching along the corridor. The door was unlocked and the old man entered carrying a plate of lamb stew, with a hunk of bread on the side, which he handed to Martin.

Behind him was the other man who covered Martin with the revolver while the food was being passed to him. The old man then retired closing the door behind him. The other remained, standing against the door.

'You speak German?' he asked in that language.

'Yes.'

'Provided you behave yourself and provided other people are sensible, you will not be hurt. Indeed, I hope it will not be necessary to keep you here too long. But that depends on other people ...'

'Which other people?'

'Those who have your safety at heart.'

'May I ask why I've been kidnapped and am being held against my will?'

'It is better that you should not ask stupid questions. You yourself have behaved criminally and could receive very severe punishment. It is well that you should remember that.'

'These other people you refer to, are you in touch with them at this moment?'

The man clearly regarded the question as irrelevant, if not impertinent.

'I am not here to answer your questions. I tell you only that you will be safe and freed before many days if everyone behaves sensibly. If they do not behave sensibly, it will be bad for you ... I will tell you, too, that only six people know where you are and none of them are your friends.'

His lip curled in a cold smile. 'You cannot escape and no one will rescue you, so do not have such hopes.'

He knocked on the door behind his back and the old man opened it, and came across to take Martin's plate.

'I'd like to wash,' Martin said.

'That is permitted. Come.'

Martin followed him into the corridor but was then made to walk in front. There was an alcove on the opposite side a few yards down with a sink and cold tap. In a deeper recess beside it was a w.c. The man watched him while he made use of both facilities.

'Do you supply towels?' Martin asked, shaking his dripping hands and head.

'Use blanket. Or your own clothing. This is not a hotel.'

'Apparently!'

A couple of minutes later, Martin had been locked back in his cell. He did not imagine he would receive any more visits before morning.

It now seemed that he had not been kidnapped in order to be subjected to further interrogation, which was what he had been expecting. From the recent conversation he had had, it was reasonably plain that he was being held to ransom. Obviously not a money ransom. So what?

He lay down on the hard bed and set about revising his ideas. He was reminded of the sort of court case, all too familiar to him, which changes its face with every fresh witness so that the advocate on the shifting side finds himself discarding lines of approach almost as soon as they have been hatched in his mind.

The only difference being that this was no forensic exercise, but, rather, a deadly game of chess in which he was a captured pawn.

His mind fastened on to the one element in his predicament which seemed to favour him. The fact that they needed him to stay alive.

Might it not be possible to exploit it in devising an escape plan? It was along this line that he must concentrate his thinking.

CHAPTER TWELVE

Peacock guided his wife through the crowded foyer of the Royal Opera House. He had booked a table for dinner at a restaurant called Lorenzo's not far away and was anxious to get there ahead of others who were similarly bound. When he had waited until eleven o'clock for his dinner, he did not welcome a further delay occasioned by too many people trying to order at the same moment.

'Enjoy it?' he asked, as they struggled out on to the pavement.

'I thought the sets were hideous.'

'One doesn't go to Covent Garden primarily for the scenery,' he observed dryly.

'And the tenor hadn't the first notion of how to act.'

'But he sang well, I thought.'

'I suppose so. Except I found myself distracted by that absurd get-up he was wearing.'

'What about the orchestra, didn't you think they played magnificently? The third act overture completely melted me.'

'It always annoys me that one can't see them. I'd like to be able to watch them playing.'

Peacock sighed. He enjoyed opera very much and maintained a quite unjustifiable hope that his wife, never the easiest of people to please, would one day succumb and share his delight. It was clear, however, that that day had still not arrived. Be the truth known it never would, but Celia Peacock preferred to accompany him and carp afterwards, than to declare robustly that opera was not for her and that he could find another companion for his visits to Covent Garden. This way she was able to appear sweetly unselfish as well as make amusing capital out of the evening when later describing it to friends at cocktail parties.

'A good dinner will soon make you forget the scenery *and* the invisible orchestra *and* the tenor's unbecoming outfit,' he said hopefully as they crossed the street. 'I've already decided what I'm going to have. I shall start with moules and go on to the braised duckling with the chestnuts and cherries.'

'I'm sure it's not called braised duckling on the menu,' she said in a tone that never strayed far from the sarcastic.

'It isn't, but that's how Lorenzo always describes it when one asks. What are you going to have?'

'I haven't an idea. As a matter of fact I'm not particularly hungry.'

'You will be once we're there.'

'Is it very much farther? I can never remember which street it's in.'

'Just round the next corner.'

'Thank goodness for that. These shoes are not made for pounding about London's pavements.'

'I didn't think it was worth fighting for a cab. It's less than five minutes walk and it's rather a nice evening, too.'

Celia Peacock made no reply but put on her martyred expression. She had never been anything but spoilt, and resentment, which had begun to corrode her outlook soon after marriage when she discovered that her husband's job had stronger claims on his time than she had, now coursed through her veins.

They arrived at the restaurant and went immediately to their table after she had said she did not want a cocktail first. Peacock had sighed again and told them to bring him a large Vodka Martini at once.

He had downed most of this, and they were studying the huge menu with its indecipherable purple writing on the parchment-like paper, when Lorenzo himself came bustling up.

'Ah, Mrs Peacock and Mr Peacock, how nice to see you again! You are both well, I hope?'

'Very well and hungry, too,' Peacock said with matching bonhomie, while his wife smiled distantly.

'They give you the message when you arrive, Mr Peacock?'

'No, nobody's given me any message. What message are you talking about?'

'You were to ring your office as soon as you came. I told Maria to tell you when you checked your coats.'

'We didn't have anything to check in. I'd better go and do it now.' He gave his wife an appeasing look. 'You order for me, dear. You know what I want. I shan't be gone long.'

It would not take him more than a minute to get through to the duty officer, who would be sitting in the cheerless first floor room which had a poky bedroom off it.

'Peacock here,' he announced when the connection was made, and then gave the code number by which he identified himself when calling from outside. A number which was regularly changed.

'Sorry to disturb your evening,' a rather nervous voice said at the other end of the line, 'but I think you ought to come back. Something pressing and important has blown up in one of your operations.'

'It can't wait till morning?'

'No.'

'And you can't deal with it?'

'I think you'd want to handle it yourself.'

'Very well. I'll come straight away.'

It had been an unsatisfactory exchange, but as much as could be safely said on an open line. Moreover, he was now faced with the infinitely trickier part of breaking the news to his wife. And he knew it would be no good reminding her that not many minutes ago she had declared herself not to be very hungry.

She looked up with a quizzical expression as he returned to the table.

'You were right,' she said, with a chilly little smile, 'looking at the menu has given me an appetite.'

'I'm afraid I shall have to go back to the office,' he remarked in a resigned and apologetic note.

'What, tonight?' she asked indignantly.

'Now.'

'Well, really!'

'Why don't you have your dinner and I'll try and get back as soon as I can?'

'That's about the least constructive suggestion you could have made. You've no idea how long you'll be, and I certainly have no intention of sitting here while the waiters go off duty and I'm left alone with a cup of cold coffee.'

He shrugged helplessly.

'I'm terribly sorry. But it's something pretty important that won't wait till morning.'

She seemed about to make some withering reply, but with a petulant toss of the head she rose from the table and stalked from the restaurant.

Peacock followed her, pausing only to explain to Lorenzo.

Luck was with him and a taxi drew up to decant its passengers as they stepped outside. He helped her in and gave their Kensington address to the driver. She was gazing out of the opposite window as it pulled away.

Almost immediately another taxi came up and he got in.

Burnett, the young duty officer, sprang up from the desk as soon as Peacock entered the room. Though he had little doubt that he had done the right thing, it required a certain amount of temerity to suggest to someone of Peacock's seniority that he should come back to the office without delay. The whole idea of the duty officer was that he should deal with what he could, leave non-urgent matters until the morning and, only in exceptional circumstances, send for one of the heads of section.

'It's this cable from Brian Hart in Istanbul,' he said, handing the document to Peacock while anxiously watching his expression.

That this particular operation had curdled still further did not surprise Peacock. He had guessed as much coming along in the taxi. It was the extent of the deterioration which mattered.

With the air of judicial calm he always assumed in front of junior officers, he read the cable. It ran:

'Arrived Istanbul hour ago. Ainsworth in opposition hands. Believed to be in city or vicinity, but no clue as to where held. Opposition will release him in exchange for our German friend. Suggest this beyond consideration. Meanwhile all efforts maintained to find Ainsworth, but locals not very helpful. Please advise immediately. Hart.'

To give himself time to think, Peacock glanced at the other data on the cable. It had been decoded an hour before and sent across by special messenger. Brian Hart had despatched it at ten minutes to eight that evening. It was now a quarter past eleven.

He turned and left the duty officer's room, as he did not wish to betray his feelings to the young man who was observing him intently.

It was rare enough for him to have feelings to betray in regard to the execution of one of his meticulously planned operations. But now he was actually experiencing a sense of alarm. He was the person ultimately responsible for Martin Ainsworth's safety. And if anything happened to him all hell would be let loose twice over. There would be no question of hushing this up, the way one could where one of his own professionals got caught with his trousers down. No question, either, in this case of putting out some bland emollient statement of semi-truths whose effect would be publicly to repudiate Ainsworth's involvement in anything for which the service was responsible.

If the operation had failed and Ainsworth had fallen into hostile hands, it would be disastrous enough. But the operation had not failed, it had succeeded, but at the last minute triumph had been neutralised by Ainsworth's kidnapping. It was this which made it that much more bitter.

And the price of Ainsworth's release would be to turn success into abject failure. A failure whose repercussions would be fully exploited by the other side. A failure, moreover, which would involve the almost certain death of one person . . .

Peacock entered the room and switched on the lights. He walked slowly across and flung himself down in the black leather arm-chair kept for visitors. He must sit and think a while. Just as the duty officer had decided to involve him, so he must now decide whether to involve his own superiors. He prayed he could avoid this. It all depended on whether he could see any chink of light in this blackest of black situations. Furthermore, he had not much time . . .

He got up and went round to his desk where he drafted a short reply to Hart's cable. It read:

'Ainsworth must be found. Meanwhile temporise with opposition.'

And as an afterthought, he added:

'Keep German friend safest.'

He took it along to the duty officer for immediate encoding and despatch to Istanbul.

Then he returned to his room and after switching out the main light sat down once more in the arm-chair, which now stood in the peripheral shadow cast by his desk lamp.

CHAPTER THIRTEEN

It would be an exaggeration to say that sunlight was pouring into Martin's cell when he awoke the next morning. On the other hand it was apparent from the degree and nature of the light which filtered through the small, barred window that the sun was shining.

He looked at his watch and saw that the time was seven o'clock. With almost neurotic fierceness he rewound the watch.

Though the bed had been anything but comfortable—it was hard, narrow and without a pillow—he had slept soundly and felt remarkably refreshed. He was also more than ever determined to effect his escape. It might take him a day to study the routine of his guards—he had yet to find out if the two he had seen were the sole occupants of the house—but he was now even more confident that their need to keep him alive was a factor in his favour.

As he lay gazing up at the ceiling in thought, his mind playing over various possibilities like a garden hose over an herbaceous border, his attention became focused on the window. It was only about eighteen inches by ten and barred, as well, so that there was no hope of escape that way. All he could see was a small segment of sky. Nevertheless it would be useful to know what lay on the other side of the outer wall of his cell.

He reckoned that if he propped the bed on end and then clambered on top, he would easily be able to see out. It was something he decided to do, but first he would wait until one or other of his guards had visited him. He thought it likely this would be quite soon. He hoped they would bring him food, but they would almost certainly come and make sure he was still alive and kicking.

And so it turned out. About half an hour later, he heard footsteps on the stairs and along the stone corridor. They paused outside his door. A key was turned, two bolts were shot and the door swung open to reveal the same two as the previous night.

The old man was carrying a small tray on which was a small cup of black coffee, a chunk of grey bread and, flowing all over the place, some honey. The other man stood in the doorway covering Martin with a revolver.

Martin had swung his legs off the bed and was in a sitting position. He noticed that the old man was careful not to mask the line of fire nor to come so close that Martin could grab hold of him.

On the other hand, with initiative on his side, it ought to be possible to make a sudden dive and hold the old man in front of him as a shield before the other could fire, always hoping that he would in any case be reluctant to do this. However, the thing to do was to allow them to believe that thoughts of escape never entered his mind, and this meant patience. They must be induced to become less vigilant. Familiarity must breed laxity.

'I'd like to shave,' Martin said, as he started to eat his breakfast.

'Not possible. Nor necessary.'

He had not shaved since the hotel in Sofia the day before yesterday and his face was covered by a grizzled stubble.

'At least you can let me wash!'

'Wash, O.K.'

'Is there any point in my asking you what's happening?'

'I tell you last night.'

'I was wondering whether anything further had happened since last night?'

'Perhaps today, if your friends are sensible. If they are not sensible ...' He completed the sentence with a small explosive sound with his lips.

Martin ate on in silence. The bread was better than it looked, the honey was delicious and the thick, strong coffee was as fine a stimulant as he could have wished for.

Whether it was the wit-sharpening effect of the coffee or sheer wishful thinking he did not know, but he somehow had an impression that the man was not as sure of himself as he appeared. There were tiny indications of tension about him, as though he feared something disagreeable might suddenly transpire.

If Martin did read the signs aright, discovery must surely be what he was afraid of. That he was a Bulgarian was a reasonable inference—there was a large minority of them in western Turkey—and that meant he was a foreigner operating well outside the law of the country whose hospitality he enjoyed. Martin could imagine that the Turkish authorities would crack down heavily and indiscriminately on anyone they caught who was involved in such activities.

So here was a second factor which might be turned to his advantage. The man's fear of his own situation.

No further words were exchanged and as soon as he had finished his food, the cup and plate were removed and he was locked up again. It was only after the footsteps had died away that he remembered he had not had his promised wash. He shrugged. His appearance was of no great importance at the moment and the coffee had achieved more than cold water in bringing his mind fully awake.

He got up off the bed and pulled it out from the wall. Then picking it up at one end he placed it like a step-ladder against the outside wall, so that the top rested about four feet below the bottom of the window.

There were metal strips across the frame of the bed and he decided that they would just about take his weight individually provided he went up like a spry mariner and did not allow his weight to linger on any one strip.

He put his right foot on the strip nearest the floor and tested it. It bent alarmingly. He found, however, that if he placed his foot not in the middle but at one end where the strips were nailed to the wooden frame of the bed, there was much less give. Accordingly, he would have to make his climb both rapidly and with feet well apart.

Standing at the base of his improvised ladder and gripping the sides firmly with both hands, he mentally enacted his climb. Then before he had time to think further and nurture inhibitions, he shinned up. As he neared the top, he reached up and grasped the bars across the window. A second later he was standing on the edge of the bed against the wall and was looking out.

Because of the shape of the window and of the siting of the bars over it, he was unable to see what lay immediately beneath. In fact, all he could see was a jumble of small houses with patches of uneven ground between them.

There were some children playing on one of the patches and farther over to the right a tiny crescent of street was in view. He was able to see such a minimal amount of this that no one remained in sight for more than a few seconds as they passed to and fro.

The house nearest to him had a basement area, also with barred windows. At one of them he could see the head of an agitated cat as it struggled to get out.

'So you're a prisoner, too,' he murmured sympathetically.

He had a final look around before climbing back down. The bed had already slipped once in ominous fashion and he did not want it to slide away beneath him. Apart from the tell-tale noise. he might also end up with a sprained ankle or fractured wrist.

The one thing he had learnt from his reconnaissance was that the ground was lower on this side of the house. He had entered at ground level on the other side, descended a flight of stairs and was still at ground level.

Since, however, there could be no question of escaping via the window, he could not see that the information availed him very much. Nevertheless, it had given some point to the exploit. He had done something positive: he had learnt something as a result.

He put the bed back where it came from and sat on it. Then he noticed that it had marked the wall where one end had rested. He wondered whether his guards would see the marks next time they entered the cell. He hoped not, though there was nothing he could do about it. Some plaster from the wall had also rubbed off on the bed. This he was able to brush off quite easily.

The rest of the morning passed with painful slowness. He had nothing to do save think, and he soon discovered that his thoughts were circumscribed by the physical fact of his incarceration. For the first time in his life he felt a kinship with all those detained without trial and held in solitary confinement. Previously, they had been an amorphous group one read about in newspapers and sometimes prayed for in church, but now he was one of them. He wondered at what stage hope was finally extinguished. Perhaps it never was this side of death or insanity.

He turned his mind once more to thoughts of his own escape ... He would observe the routine when they brought him his next meal, with the idea of making a getaway at suppertime.

Shortly after noon, he heard approaching footsteps and a few seconds later, the door was unlocked and his two guards entered. As before, the old one brought in the food while the other covered Martin with his revolver.

He sat quietly on the bed and made no attempt to move. Let them think he was sunk in apathetic despair. The old man pushed the tray across the floor towards Martin's feet. On it was a bowl of soup with pieces of vegetable floating around on the surface, and beside the bowl another hunk of the same grey bread.

The two men watched him eat. He made no effort to talk until he had finished.

'I want to wash,' he said, standing up.

The man with the revolver nodded and motioned him out into the passage. Martin was dismayed to notice how careful he was not to make himself vulnerable to sudden attack and how he moved to prevent the very manoeuvre which his prisoner was contemplating for a later occasion. Nevertheless, Martin again had the impression of hidden uneasiness on the man's part. But leaving that aside, it was a question of escaping that way or not at all. Everything would hinge on the man's degree of reluctance to use his revolver—and Martin could only trust that he had made the right assumption about that.

He had as good a wash as was possible with cold water and a small cracked piece of non-lather soap. The lavatory, which was next to the tap and sink, had no window and no latch on its door. It reminded Martin of those at his public school, where the doors were not even allowed to be shut. Though this had been for reasons other than security. His guard raised no protest when Martin closed the door. He could not escape and, as he had not attempted to commit suicide in his cell, there was no reason to believe he would try there.

When Martin emerged, the man had moved and was standing outside the cell door. He backed away as Martin approached, almost as if he thought he might try and rush him. Martin, however, pretended not to notice and put on the air of one mentally pummelled into submission.

After being locked up again, he lay down on the bed and gave his mind to planning his suppertime escape.

There seemed to be two alternatives. One was to make a leap at the old man as he pushed the tray towards Martin and use him as a shield against the armed one. The other was to hurl his plate of food into the face of the man with the revolver and make a dash for it in the seconds before he could recover.

It seemed absurd, but he was not sure that the choice of plan would not turn on what he was brought for supper. A plate of cold meat in the face would be nothing like as effective as a pint of hot soup.

Given the right food for his purpose, he preferred the second plan. It had better surprise value and quicker execution. The first plan contained one large unknown factor, namely the physical strength of the old man. He might well find himself engaged in a wrestling match which would end with the other man cracking him over the head with the revolver.

No, the more he thought about it, the more he preferred the direct action plan. He must just hope that his supper would consist of some culinary napalm.

If anything, the afternoon passed more slowly than the morning and he found himself glancing at his watch every ten minutes. It seemed far longer than six hours before the patch of sky through the window turned from blue to pink to purple.

Seven o'clock came, eight, eight-thirty, but still there was no sound of approaching footsteps. Nine and ten o'clock and the silence remained unbroken.

He tried to think of all the things that might have happened. There was probably some mundane explanation, but meanwhile he was left to speculate. To speculate and to chafe, because the delay was bitterly frustrating. By now he had hoped in his most optimistic mood to be free. But free or not, the nervous tension which had been building up all afternoon should have been over, instead of which it continued to increase. His nerve ends felt as though they had been exposed and dipped in vinegar. He began to experience aches in his legs and round his shoulders, as he did after a particularly strenuous game of tennis. His brain had kept his muscles on stand-by call for too long and they were rebelling.

At midnight, he lay down on the bed and tried to make his mind a blank. It was now quite obvious that something had happened to cause normal routine to be waived. Whether it was something good or bad, he could not know. All he could do was to await morning and if no one appeared then, he would break the cell window and try and attract attention.

He thought he must have dozed off, but suddenly all his senses were alerted. At first, he was unable to identify the cause and then he heard sounds in the passage outside. Someone was definitely approaching. He sat up and fixed his eyes on the door. The two bolts were slipped back, the key was turned and the door was thrown abruptly open to reveal Mr Gursan, holding a wicked-looking little gun in his right hand.

CHAPTER FOURTEEN

For several seconds, Martin stared at him incredulously, while Mr Gursan observed *him* with a faintly sardonic expression. The eyes still gave his face an air of attractive strength. They were the eyes of a man whom experience of life had taught compassion.

One thing which definitely registered on Martin's mind at this moment was that Mr Gursan was in no way surprised to find him there. Indeed, his first words confirmed this impression.

'So! And how is my English friend from the bus? I have been looking forward to our meeting again.'

'I'm glad to see you, too,' Martin said. 'At least, I hope I have reason to do so.'

'That depends,' Mr Gursan replied disconcertingly. 'But let us go.' He stood aside to let Martin go first. 'Please do not try to escape. You will see that I have a gun and though I do not like to kill anyone, it is sometimes a regrettable necessity.' He paused before adding, 'And if it is a necessity, I do not hesitate.'

Martin could readily believe this. It confirmed one of his first impressions that he looked just the type of staunch person to have on your side in any trouble. Unhappily, at this moment, Mr Gursan was clearly not regarding them as being on the same side.

As they reached the door which led into the courtyard, it was opened from outside and Martin saw two much younger but extremely tough looking men standing by a car, whose engine was running. One of them opened the rear door and Martin got in. Mr Gursan got in beside him. The other young man came round to the other door and sat on Martin's other side.

The driver ran and opened the high wooden gates of the courtyard and closed them again after they had driven out into the street.

Martin cast a quick glance at the building in which he had spent the past twenty-seven hours. It was in darkness and appeared deserted.

'May I ask what's going on?' he said, turning to Mr Gursan as the car accelerated away in a burst of speed.

'Soon there will be plenty of time for questions,' Mr Gursan replied evenly. He said something to the man on Martin's other side who reached down and picked up a sack from the floor.

'Please, if you do not mind, I think it is better you do not see,' Mr Gursan said, as the sack was suddenly popped over Martin's head. 'Istanbul is a beautiful city, but not for you tonight.' His tone held a note of quiet authority. It was neither hostile nor friendly and Martin decided that no good would come of asking further questions. In any event there was something a bit humiliating in asking questions with your head in a sack. Instead he would listen to sounds and see whether they provided him with any clue as to where they were going.

He reckoned they drove for about ten minutes and at breakneck speed before lurching round a particularly sharp bend and braking to an abrupt halt. Indeed if it had not been for Gursan's steadying hand he would have been thrown violently forward.

'Come, I guide you,' Mr Gursan said.

They went two steps up into a building, along a corridor with a wooden floor, up a flight of stairs, along another corridor and then into a room on the right.

The door was closed behind them and he was pushed against a chair.

'Sit.'

He did so and heard a blind being drawn. Then the sack was pulled from his head and he was able to survey his surroundings.

The room had the functional appearance of a not very comfortable office. Everything looked shabby and there was a smell compounded of stale sweat and something more acrid.

Mr Gursan had seated himself behind a small desk, which had a flaking rexine top, and was watching him thoughtfully. The gun lay on the desk within comfortable reach of his right hand.

121

'And now we begin our talk, yes?' he said after Martin's wondering gaze had come to rest on him. Martin said nothing and he went on. 'You have the wisdom of silence, but eventually you must talk. You must tell me what I want to know. I know much, but there is one thing I do not know and that is why you are here.'

Martin could not help noticing how much better Mr Gursan's spoken English was on this occasion than it had been on the bus.

'Yes, just one thing I do not know and it is the most important thing of all.' Mr Gursan's eyes never left Martin's face while he was speaking. Now he made a quick scything gesture with his left hand as though to sweep away any niggling observations Martin might be about to voice. 'But before I can expect you to talk, I must tell you certain things. Things which will encourage you to tell me what I wish to know.

'First I should tell you that you are in the headquarters of a section of the Turkish Counter-Intelligence Service. I am an officer of that service, just as you, my friend, are an officer of the British Secret Intelligence Service.'

Martin shook his head. 'I'm not ...'

'Let us not play with words! You were on that bus for an "intelligence" purpose, so please do not deny it!' Martin shrugged. 'Thank you, and now I go on.' His voice, which had become sharp, resumed its even tone. 'You and others were engaged in smuggling someone from Bulgaria into Turkey. You see, I know that. It was because I knew it was going to happen that I, too, was on the bus. I wished to find out how the game was played. We do not like our country being used in that way without our knowing what is happening. Well, I found out much. In fact I found out everything except for this one thing. I do not know who it was that was rescued. I was fooled and I do not like to be fooled. And so now you are going to help me.'

The last sentence came out as a statement and not as a question, and Martin waited.

'You are going to tell me the name of the person who was rescued?'

'I don't know it,' Martin said bluntly. 'Since you know so much, you must obviously be aware that the plan went badly wrong. All I can tell you is that the intended object of rescue was an East German. A woman, But to the best of my belief, she was never got out.'

'Her name?'

'Paula Zwehl,' Martin said without any hesitation. If divulging such information was in breach of Peacock's code, that was just too bad!

Mr Gursan shook his head impatiently. 'Certainly the plan went wrong, but not as wrong as that.' He looked up with a frown and added sharply, 'It is bad if you do not tell me the truth. You can be turned over to the courts for punishment if you do not co-operate.'

Martin said nothing for a few seconds. Then he sighed. 'Perhaps it would help if I told you what I do know...'

With only a slight gloss to make it appear that he was more fool than knave, he retailed his version of events, emphasising in particular his own minor and passive rôle in the whole affair. When he had finished, Mr Gursan pursed his lips for a while. Eventually he said:

'If you have told me the truth, it seems I know much more about your operation than you.'

'I promise I've told you the truth.'

'It is possible.'

'It's certain.'

'But you must still help me.'

'If I can.'

'You have no alternative, my friend. No pleasant alternative, that is!'

Mr Gursan fell into deep thought, spinning the gun on the desk like a roulette wheel as he stared across the room through half-closed eyes. Martin waited for him to speak again. He was too conscious of his delicate situation to do or say anything which might ruffle Mr Gursan's feathers. All manner of disagreeable pressures could be brought to bear and he must just hope to avoid the worst.

It was two or more minutes before his interrogator's gaze fell once more on his face, at first distantly and then with a sudden focusing of attention.

'I have not gone to the trouble of rescuing you for nothing.' In a fiercer tone he added, 'So you will have to find out for me what I wish to know.'

'Come to that, I don't yet know whom you rescued me from,' Martin observed.

'From Gorsev of course! He is a Bulgarian merchant in this city, but he has many ties with the government in Sofia. He is clever and dangerous, but we are cleverer and we, too, can be dangerous. We know him for long time and know more about him than he would like us to know. We watch him and he thinks he watches us . . .'

'What's happened to him?'

'He was called away on urgent business tonight,' Mr Gursan said equably.

'But how did you know I was being held there?'

'We find out.' Martin waited for further explanation but none came.

'Do you know why I was being held?'

'I can guess. They were wishing to exchange you for the person who was helped to escape from their country.'

His face creased in a sudden, not entirely friendly grin. 'And now it is I who hold you in exchange for information. I do not want the body of the person, only the name. That, my friend, is what you are going to find out for me.' He picked up the gun and weighed it lovingly in the palm of his hand, then with a conjuror's dexterity held it in the next moment in his other hand pointing straight at Martin's stomach. With a laugh he laid it back on the desk.

'How and where do I start to find that out?' Martin asked without enthusiasm.

'At the office of Herold Touring Company. Your luggage is there. You will go and claim it.'

'And?'

'You will ask to speak to the manager and you will complain about the way you were left at the roadside. You will probably see the driver Hans there. He is working in the office.'

'I thought the bus started back the next morning?'

'It did, but without Hans. Hans will not be able to drive in Bulgaria again. They are very angry with him.'

'You mean he was in on the rescue plan?'

'But of course.'

'And Ali, too?'

'No, not Ali. Anyway, Ali is now on his way to Persia for a holiday. But the Bulgarians will take reprisals against the bus company, I think.'

'How was the person got out?'

'Perhaps in the luggage trailer. It is a guess.'

'But at what stage?'

'Aah! That is the whole question! If I knew at what stage, I would know who it was.'

'But was there anyone hidden in the trailer on arrival in

Istanbul?'

'No, there was not. That is where I was fooled.'

'Then how do you know anyone ever was in it?'

'I don't. But you will find out for me.'

'And if I can't?'

'There will be difficulties for you.'

'Such as?'

'You will be unable to leave the country. You may be detained for lengthy questioning ... After all, I only have your word that you have told me the truth ...'

'What about my own people, what do you think they are going to say about this? They won't be inactive all this time!'

'As you say, they are not inactive. A man called Brian Hart arrived a few hours ago from Munich. You know this Mr Hart, yes?'

'No.'

Mr Gursan frowned. 'You are either very ignorant or very stupid.' He brought his fist heavily down on the desk. 'Because to tell me lies is very stupid.'

'I'm not lying,' Martin said evenly. 'I have never heard of Brian Hart. Who is he, anyway?'

'He is a member of the British Secret Intelligence Service.'

'You seem to know a good deal about that service.'

'It is part of my job. But to answer your question, there is very little your friends can do to help you. In the first place they do not know where you are. They believe you are still in Gorsev's custody, because Gorsev has made approaches to them about an exchange.' Mr Gursan's mouth twisted in a small cynical smile. 'But it could be that they are not too keen on such an exchange. They do not want to throw away weeks of successful planning and preparation ...'

'You don't even know that it has been successful.'

'But you are going to find out for me.'

This refrain was beginning to grate on Martin's nerves. It rubbed in the fact that Mr Gursan clearly regarded him as a useful pawn to be launched into battle at his will.

Mr Gursan stretched and let out a yawn. 'And now we will go to bed. In the morning we will talk again and I will tell you what you will have to do. I will also tell you why you shouldn't have any foolish ideas in your head. Ideas about pretending to help me and then running to your friends.'

Martin glanced up sharply since this was the thought which had been occupying his mind. He could not see what control

Mr Gursan could exercise over him once he was on his own, as he would be when he went to the Herold Touring office. He could hardly be accompanied by somebody sticking a gun in his ribs.

'You will sleep here, but I think it is more comfortable than at Gorsev's. Tomorrow we will give you a razor for shaving and a fine breakfast and we shall resume our talk. O.K.?'

He went to the door and shouted something down the passage. The young man who had sat on Martin's other side in the car came in. He motioned to Martin to follow him.

'Good night, my friend,' Mr Gursan said benignly, as he returned to his desk.

As they made their way down to the basement of the building, it struck Martin how few windows there were. There had been one in Mr Gursan's office over which he had pulled a blind, but the corridors had an entirely subterranean appearance.

The room into which he was shown was also without a window and at first sight it was difficult to see why. Mr Gursan had boasted of it being more comfortable than his last place of detention. There seemed little to choose between them. This one had a hard chair, which the other had not. On the other hand it was considerably dirtier. It was lit by a grimy twenty-watt bulb screwed into the ceiling, which cast a gloom resembling that of a foggy November day in London. The only ventilation came from a grille above the door.

The young man wasted no time, but immediately departed, locking the door behind him. Martin sat down on the bed and stared mindlessly at the opposite wall. Reaction had set in and he felt numbed by exhaustion. Too much had happened in too short a space of time, most of it, moreover, belonging to a fevered realm of fantasy. Two consecutive nights locked in a different cell and the one before that spent in a field in Eastern Bulgaria. First kidnapped by one side and then by the other, as if he were the treasure in some grotesque treasure hunt.

He walked over and switched off the light. At least he had control of that in his present cell. Then he lay down on the bed and closed his eyes. But perversely sleep would not come, and his mind began to clear and focus once more on his situation.

Thinking back, he realised how vague Mr Gursan had been about the means of finding out who the escapee was. 'You will

126

go to the office of Herold Touring and claim your baggage,' he had said. What this, plus a complaint about being left behind, was expected to achieve in Mr Gursan's cause had not been explained, Martin assumed, because there was no rational explanation. Mr Gursan was proposing to use him on a general fishing expedition with the threat of disagreeable consequences if he did not make a catch. But what was to prevent him going straight to the British Consulate and demanding protection and repatriation? Mr Gursan seemed confident he could forestall such a move. Martin wondered how. At all events, it seemed that freedom of a sort was not far off.

Mr Gursan had mentioned that a Brian Hart had arrived from Munich to take charge of his end of the operation. Martin wondered if he had been one of the men who had watched the departure of the bus from outside the Hauptbahnhof. He remembered having observed two or three bystanders as the bus pulled away and having wondered if one of them was Peacock's man on the spot.

Judged by his own experience, Martin could not believe that the operation had been even partially successful, though Mr Gursan appeared to think otherwise. But being in the same line of business as Peacock meant he was devious, and being, additionally, a Turk multiplied the cells of that particular characteristic.

It was while he was reviewing in his mind the series of events which had begun with Anna Schmidt's disappearance in Sofia that he suddenly remembered two emergency telephone numbers which Peacock had given him. He had been required to memorise them and had been told to use them only in the event of direct urgency. One had been a number in Sofia which he had understood to be the private residence of someone in the embassy. The other had been an Istanbul number. When Martin had protested that he never could carry figures of this sort in his head, Peacock had supplied him with an address. He had done so with obvious reluctance and had almost told Martin to forget it immediately. It was true that he had not thought of it during the past four days, but now it suddenly broke the surface of his mind with the plop of a tiny bubble. It was the Villa Yekta at somewhere called Yeniköy which he understood to be on the western shore of the Bosporus half a dozen miles or so north of Istanbul. Peacock had been insistent that he was not to approach the villa except with enormous circumspection and that he was to try and memorise the telephone number and not go there at all.

'It so happens I can't remember the number,' Martin murmured self-defiantly.

He wondered whether Mr Gursan knew of the Villa Yekta. Shortly after this he fell asleep.

He was awakened by someone shaking his shoulder roughly. The anaemic yellow light was on and he saw from his watch that the time was half past seven. The young man standing over him indicated he should get up. Martin did so, putting on his trousers and shoes and jacket which were the only clothes he had removed. He reckoned he must smell pretty high, but that was other people's look-out, not his. He followed the young man along the passage to a dingy room containing two wash-basins and a w.c. in a row. There was a razor and some shaving cream beside one of the basins, as well as a rough towel. He looked at himself in the heavily scratched mirror which was attached to the wall between the two basins. He had not shaved for three days and it was going to hurt, especially as the razor blade had a cheap, tinny appearance.

Ten minutes later, he had scraped off most of his beard, though as he ran his hand over his face he could feel small isolated tufts which had escaped attention. However, there was no doubt that a shave, even a bad one, benefited the morale. He towelled his head vigorously and twisting one end round his finger cleaned his teeth as well.

On returning to his cell, escorted by the young man who had stayed to witness his ablutions, he found a tray with his breakfast. There was yoghourt, coffee and some round oatmeal cakes which were flavoured with honey. He wondered whether this was the regular breakfast for the Counter-Intelligence Service's overnight guests or whether he was the recipient of special treatment. He had not quite finished the meal when the door opened and Mr Gursan came in.

'You enjoy your breakfast, yes?'

'It's very good.'

'Turkish coffee is best in world.'

'And the yoghourt, too.'

'Also very good,' Mr Gursan agreed, nodding.

'Now, if you have finished, we go to my office. We still have things to talk about and the days are not long enough.'

Although Mr Gursan had not shaved, he had sprayed himself with some preparation which made him smell like a bed of sweet peas. Martin wondered whether he had done so to subdue his own pungent body odours or to keep Martin's at bay.

By daylight, his office looked shabbier than it had the previous night. The blind was up but there was nothing to be seen through the window which was of frosted glass.

As soon as they were seated, Mr Gursan wasted no time in preliminaries.

'I have told you what I wish you to find out for me. I have told you that things will be made difficult for you if you fail me. I now tell you that I give you forty-eight hours to do what I want.' He watched Martin's face as though challenging him to protest.

'You said last night I was to go to the Herold Touring office and demand to see the manager. Supposing I do that, supposing, even, I see and talk to Hans, it won't necessarily bring me any closer to discovering what you want to know. So what do I do next?'

'I do not mind how you find the information, I am only interested in the answer. It is up to you.'

So Martin had been right, Mr Gursan did not have any ideas on how he was to set about his hopeless assignment. He was to be slipped his lead and told to search with less scent than a police dog.

'You have no suggestions as to where I should seek apart from Herold Touring?'

'None.'

'And what makes you think you can rely on me to find out what you want within forty-eight hours?'

Mr Gursan nodded as though the question was a particularly good one. 'Last night you tell me you are a lawyer. That I did not know, but I did know that you are an English gentleman. You have heard that I speak good English, yes?'

'Extremely good.'

'I spent several years studying in England, that is why. I came to like the English people then, to respect their regard for fair play and their sense of honour. These things, I read, are not now so strong as they were. Perhaps that is so, I do not know, but they are still strong in people of your generation.'

Martin listened without giving away his thoughts which were largely compounded of astonishment that Mr Gursan could be making an old-fashioned appeal to his honour, in this instance not to fail the Turkish Counter-Intelligence Service. He was almost dismayingly naïve.

'So,' Mr Gursan went on, 'I believe you will do as I say.'

Martin shrugged as if to indicate that the situation was too absurd for words. 'Because if you don't, it is not only you, but others who will suffer.'

'I don't understand.'

'Two of your compatriots are in serious trouble and only you can help them.'

'Yes?' His throat suddenly constricted, as he felt himself being irresistibly drawn into a trap which was about to close. 'Two persons named Heckstrap and Lingman.'

'Are they the boy and girl who gave me a lift in their car?'

'I thought you would recognise their names.'

'Why do you say they are in serious trouble?'

'They were found wandering on a military base. They could have been spying . . .'

'But that's nonsense! Why didn't you tell me about this last night when I mentioned that I'd been given a ride by these two and told you how one of the thugs who kidnapped me cut the girl's wrist with his knife?'

'Last night was not a suitable time for telling.'

'Anyway, where are they now?'

'They are detained. How long they remain in prison depends on you! You see, my friend, they also described how they had given a lift to an Englishman and how he had been running from trouble and how grateful he was to them for their help.'

'Let me get this straight,' Martin said with an edge to his voice. 'Provided I find out what you want, these two will be released. But if I fail, they won't. Is that it?'

Mr Gursan smiled in a melancholy way. 'I fear it is that. But I know you will succeed, because it is an affair of honour for you. These two young people helped you and now they need your help in return. An Englishman does not fail in those circumstances.'

Martin felt at that moment he would gladly chain Peacock and Mr Gursan together and drop them in a sack into the Bosporus. But anger and frustration were not going to help him at this juncture. Mr Gursan had him nailed down and knew it.

'And I have just forty-eight hours?'

Mr Gursan nodded. 'From nine o'clock this morning.'

'And where do I report?'

'Telephone this number from the Sirkeci railway station and a car will come for you.' He wrote a number on a piece of paper and passed it across the desk. 'After calling, you must wait where the taxis pick up their passengers.'

'If I succeed,' Martin said after a short silence, 'will you pay me a bonus?'

Mr Gursan frowned. 'I do not understand. Bonus? What sort of bonus?'

'Will you not only release my two friends, but will you also see that the young thugs who kidnapped me are suitably dealt with? Not for what they did to me, but for what they did to Miss Lingman and to the car?'

It sounded funny referring to Rache as Miss Lingman. And it was now plain where Heck had got his name.

'It is possible,' Mr Gursan replied judicially. 'But first you have to succeed ...'

CHAPTER FIFTEEN

The Herold Touring office was in a side street not far from the Blue Mosque and it was outside here that Mr Gursan stopped the car and directed him to his destination.

'Don't forget, my friend, you have only'—he glanced at the fat watch on his left wrist—'forty-seven hours from now.'

Then Martin was standing alone in the cross currents of several streams of tourists making their way to the Mosque or back to their coaches or to the Saint Sophia museum a stone's throw away.

For a few seconds he felt as bemused as a long-term prisoner after the heavy doors have been closed behind him on the morning of his release. He stood there in the warm sunshine, gazing about him while he succumbed to a flood of conflicting emotions.

Cars honked, tourists bustled, the locals lounged, but he was hardly aware of the pulsating scene until an old man forced himself under Martin's notice. He had the carefully cultivated whine of the beggar and was pushing a small wheelchair in which sat a boy of about five with horribly deformed feet. The old man pointed at the feet and held out his hand. Martin felt in his pocket and produced a coin. He had no idea what it was, but the old man snatched at it and moved away.

Martin began walking in the opposite direction. It was not the way Mr Gursan had indicated, but he decided first to circle the area abutted by these two vast monuments, which stood to the turbulent history of the city, their minarets reaching starkly upwards. Saint Sophia was now a museum, and he recalled it had originally been built as a church by the Emperor Justinian, only for it to be turned into a mosque several centuries later after one of the many conquests the city had undergone. And then in recent times when rights of ownership had once more been vociferously disputed, that modern Solomon, Kemal Ataturk, had ordained it should belong to neither sect, but should be preserved as a museum.

Some yards farther on he paused and looked out over the rolling hills on which Istanbul had been built, and across the sparkling waters of the Golden Horn and the Bosporus which divided it into three. Üsküdar on the Asian side of the Bosporus lay in the distance. On the western shore was Beyoglu separated by the Golden Horn from the district called Eminünü where he was now standing. It was somewhere in Beyoglu that Mr Gursan had his headquarters.

He thought, as his gaze ranged over the middle distance, that he could identify the mosque which he had noticed not far from where he had spent the night. Going across to a stall, he bought a cheap plan of the city, but then found difficulty in escaping without purchasing any of the tawdry souvenirs which the owner was far more interested in selling. Eventually, he walked away with the villainous looking stall-holder still producing beads and pointed slippers with furry bobbles and assorted brass nick-nacks in an effort to break down his resistance.

At a safe distance he paused and sat on a seat in the shadow of a small dusty tree. Opening out the plan, he looked for Yeniköy and found it on the western bank of the Bosporus about half-way between Istanbul and its entrance to the Black Sea. He refolded the plan and put it in his pocket.

The more he thought about it, the less attracted he was by the prospect of appearing in the Herold Touring office. Mr Gursan had suggested it because to him it provided a starting point. And, anyway, Mr Gursan had made it all too plain that he was interested only in results. How they were obtained was not his concern. But as Martin saw it, the last thing he wanted to do was to notify his own side of his whereabouts. In forty-eight hours time, the position might be different, but if he was to try and help Heck and Rache, then the fewer people who knew his movements the better. He could hardly expect Peacock or Hart to view their release as a top priority, but for him it was no less. Mr Gursan had judged him aright about that. Heck and Rache had succoured him when he was most in need and as a result they had suffered atrociously. It was unthinkable that his chief preoccupation should not now be their release. That he had confidence in Mr Gursan keeping his side of the bargain served only to enhance his determination.

But Mr Gursan did not appear to know of the Villa Yekta, so he had proposed the Herold Touring office as the starting point of Martin's quest—simply because there was no other he could think of. Perhaps he imagined that Martin would receive the returned prodigal's reception, would be briefed on everything which had happened and then be given an opportunity to slip out to a telephone...

He could not exactly say why, but Martin knew that if he was going to find out what Mr Gursan was waiting to hear and if, moreover, he was going to impart that information, then he would have to unearth it by his own endeavour, and not be told it by Hart or anyone else, unlikely though this might be. He supposed it was tied up with that same sense of honour which Mr Gursan had discoursed about. As a boy he had climbed trees in a neighbour's orchard and taken fruit, but it would never have occurred to him to steal apples or plums from the greengrocer's shop. Both were stealing in the eyes of the law, but one had seemed perfectly excusable and the other had not. And he still felt the same way. He tried to analyse the reason for this difference and decided it had to do with trust. Stealing from the shop would have involved a breach of trust, and a degree of deceit, which taking from the tree did not. In the same way, it would be impossible to pass on to Mr Gursan any information handed to him by Hart, even to save Heck and Rache. But if he found that information out for himself, he would have a clear conscience about disclosing it.

So it was a good thing that Mr Gursan had not mentioned the Villa Yekta. It was a reasonable inference that he did not know of its significance, probably not even its existence.

He looked at his watch and saw that the time was half past ten. He decided to find a taxi and drive out to Yeniköy.

CHAPTER SIXTEEN

Brian Hart yawned. He had not had much sleep since his arrival in Istanbul the previous evening. He was sitting in the small first floor room which was above the front office of Herold Touring.

Hans was standing at the window which looked out at the rear.

Hart clenched his jaws against a further yawn and made an exasperated noise.

'There's going to be all hell to pay if Ainsworth comes to any harm,' Hart said.

Hans shrugged. He was not the man's keeper. It was not his fault that Ainsworth had gone rushing off into the darkness of a Bulgarian night. If he could think of any useful suggestions he would make them, but for the moment he had none. The operation had been successful even if a number of things had gone badly wrong. As far as he was concerned, the thing which had gone most wrong was the disclosure of his complicity in the escape plan. He had hoped that could be avoided, but it was clearly impossible once the link in the chain represented by Anna Schmidt had broken.

'When did you discover that the Turks had a man on the bus?' he asked idly.

'Gursan, you mean? Not until last night when I got here. Our man in post recognised him when he was leaving the bus. That's not his real name, of course.'

'Where exactly does he fit in?'

'I imagine he was holding a watching brief. Another reason why we've reached the end of this particular little run. It's been well and truly over-exposed.'

The two men were talking in German which Hart spoke as fluently as English.

He gazed at Hans' back and wondered how he would be able to make further use of him. He was good. He had initiative, a strong nerve and, above all, a well guarded tongue. He also happened to like the money which his work for Hart brought him. In view of the risks, he had been promised an extra large emolument for this operation. On the whole, Hart reckoned he had earned every mark, though his lack of interest in Ainsworth's fate was irksome. He might at least pretend to be helpful even if he was unable to be.

'I suppose his suitcase is still here?'

'Mmn?'

'Ainsworth's suitcase. Is it downstairs?'

'As far as I know.'

'If anyone comes for it, I want to know immediately. It can be handed over and the person taking it is to be tailed. Actually, I've already arranged for anyone inquiring after Ainsworth to be treated the same way.'

'I don't suppose anyone will be so silly as to do that.'

'Depends on what sort of motive they have.'

Hart's opposite number in Istanbul was a man named Tillotson and to him had fallen the task of organising the search for Ainsworth. He was doing so with a certain degree of ill-grace since he had not welcomed Hart's swooping arrival on his territory, nor the peremptory tone of a cable he had received from Peacock which seemed to imply that Ainsworth's disappearance was his fault. His masters did not seem to appreciate that Istanbul was one of the easiest cities in the world to disappear in. Its topography, its multi-racial character and its labyrinthine construction of streets all favoured the person who wished to go underground for a while and equally those who went in for kidnapping.

At this moment, Tillotson was in the back-room of a small café near Taksim Square asking questions about the recent movements of Gorsev, who had disappeared from his usual haunts twenty-four hours previously and who had been sending him messages indicating that he could arrange for Ainsworth's safe delivery at a price. The price was a human one, on to which Gorsev had tacked a sum in Turkish lire equivalent to about £2,000. Tillotson had no doubt into whose pocket that would find its way were it ever to be paid.

But now Gorsev had, metaphorically, gone off the air and nothing had been heard from him during the past twelve hours. And despite Tillotson's best endeavours, no one seemed to have any idea where he was.

It exemplified the difficulty of working in Istanbul where someone could vanish for ever with no more than a ripple of insubstantial rumour to mark his passing.

Tillotson rose. He was due to meet Hart back at the office in a quarter of an hour to discuss the next move.

At that moment, the one thing which he and Hart shared was an intense annoyance with Peacock for having ever employed Martin Ainsworth on the operation. They had never met Martin and knew no more than that he was a successful and reputable barrister, but he was the cause of a great deal of trouble and that was enough.

It was an unreasonable annoyance; but then if you worked perpetually in the shadows you were apt to see everything in arcane dimensions.

One thing only could have added to Tillotson's exasperation and that would have been the knowledge that Peacock had mentioned the Villa Yekta to Martin. That would really have exploded him like an underwater mine.

He reckoned his use of the villa to be the best kept secret in Turkey.

CHAPTER SEVENTEEN

The road to Yeniköy clung for most of its way to the shoreline of the Bosporus. It was an attractive drive with the blue waters of that strategically sensitive waterway on one side and a green hillside on the other. The road itself was immediately flanked by a succession of villas, some of which were small modern cubes and others vast ornamental edifices which belonged to an age of pashas and carriages.

From time to time they would pass a lido where children were happily splashing in the water or a small yacht basin where the masts of the boats would be swaying violently, in the wash caused by the passing ferries which zig-zagged about the channel like bees in search of pollen.

They had just passed the sturdy battlements of the castle of Rumeli Hisar when the driver turned to find out where Martin wished to be put down. That is to say, taking both hands off the steering-wheel, he raised his arms in a helpless gesture, at the same time looking round at Martin, who nodded urgently. The car came to an immediate juddering halt. There followed a haggle over the price and a further plaint on the driver's part over something which Martin failed to fathom. Eventually, he drove off wearing an expression of resigned disgust.

There were a few scattered shops in the area, among them a

café. Martin went and sat at a table on the pebbled terrace at
the side of the café and ordered a yoghourt. When the girl
brought it to him, he asked her if she spoke English. She
smiled and shook her head. A few moments later, however, an
older woman, who could have been the girl's mother, came
up.

'You wish?' she asked, surveying him with dark suspicion.

'Villa Yekta?' he said, and was relieved to notice that her
expression cleared. Perhaps she thought he had made an im-
proper suggestion to her daughter.

'Go there!' She pointed along the road. 'On right.' She gestured vigorously with her right hand. 'One kilometre.' Here
she flung her arms wide in a determined effort to convey distance.

Martin thanked her and ordered another yoghourt. He had
just finished this when one of the ferries, which ply up and
down the Bosporus, pulled into the landing-stage which
adjoined the café and a couple of dozen passengers poured off.
Most of them made straight for the café and took up all the
unoccupied tables. Martin got up to leave, spurred by hearing
a number of them speaking English. They were obviously
tourists, but he did not wish to run the risk of becoming involved with strangers, especially fellow countrymen.

He had covered about three quarters of a kilometre when
the road, which had been running close beside the water,
curved away to the left and a number of well-spaced villas
came between it and the shoreline. He slowed his pace a
fraction and got ready to observe as much detail as he could
without giving an appearance of unnatural curiosity.

The fourth property along was hidden by a twelve foot wall
and it was impossible to see so much as a gable. A small green
gate let into the wall had 'Villa Yekta' written on it in neat
white letters. Beside the gate was a bell push. Not until he had
come level with the next villa did he stop and look back,
assuming the air of someone interested in gauging how far he
has walked.

He had been puzzled at not seeing any entrance which would
admit a car, but now he noticed for the first time that there
was a double garage built against the hillside on the opposite
side of the road. It had a small carved-out oval of space in
front of its doors to enable a car to park off the road on
entering or leaving. But now the doors were closed.

Martin crossed the road and, after making sure that he was

not being observed, began to clamber up between the trees which covered the sharply rising hillside. He reckoned that he should not have to climb very far in order to be able to see over the top of the villa's surrounding wall.

After about fifty yards, he paused and, leaning gratefully against a tree, looked back. It was better than he could have expected and he was able to see the complete lay-out.

The villa itself was medium size and of bizarre design which he could only have described as squat baronial gothic. It stood in about an acre of ground, most of it lawn, which sloped gently down to the water. He was looking at what was obviously the blind side of the building. There were a number of windows, all of them covered by dark green shutters. Of life there was not a single sign.

He clambered down, making his slithering emergence on to the road only when he was sure there was no one within sight in either direction. After dusting himself down, he set off at a brisk pace. It was clear what his next step had to be, namely to examine the other side of the house from the water.

After going the best part of a mile, he came upon what he was looking for. One of the moorings which dotted the shoreline and which advertised boats for hire. This one was close to a brand new hotel of modest size and appearance. Two men were sitting at the farther end of the little harbour mending a fishing net. One of them sprang up hopefully as Martin approached.

'You like ride in boat?' Martin nodded. 'I have good boat. I give you fine ride.'

'How much?'

'One hundred lire.'

'Too much.' He was not going to pay £5 for a half hour ride in a motor boat.

'Ninety-five.'

'Fifty.'

The man made a face designed to impress Martin that injustice was his permanent lot, but, nevertheless, moved with alacrity to prepare the boat.

It was a long, narrow craft with an outboard motor at one end. Martin sat in the middle on a purple cushion and his pilot nestled beside the outboard. As soon as they were clear of all the moored boats, Martin indicated the direction in which he wanted to be taken. Luckily the man seemed content to hug the shoreline.

It did not take more than a few minutes to reach the Villa Yekta, which was readily identifiable from the water, and Martin positioned himself to get the fullest view possible. After they had gone by, he examined in his mind's eye the plate on which his impressions had been recorded.

There had been a small pontoon landing-stage. The wall ran down to the water's edge on both sides of the garden. (It must have been built by someone with an obsession about privacy.) And the windows on this side of the house, though not shuttered, all had blinds pulled down over them. Indeed, the whole place had the air of being completely deserted. But so, too, for that matter, had the villa next to it, which made Martin thoughtful. If he was to take a closer look at Villa Yekta, the next door property might provide the best vantage point for this.

After chugging along the shoreline for a further mile, they made a great sweep out towards the middle of the channel and headed back.

Martin watched a small freighter slowly overtake them. She was unladen and her propeller, which was partially visible, lazily thrashed the water, as she headed towards the Black Sea. Two sailors were leaning on the deck rail, looking at him. Then one of them waved and he waved back. Not long after, they were no more than indistinguishable specks. He felt it was symbolic of some aspect of man's situation, but was not sure what. At that moment, their life seemed infinitely preferable to his own, though he realised it had its tougher side.

It was just after half past one when they arrived back at their starting point and his boatman put him ashore.

He remembered having passed a small restaurant about a quarter of a mile back along the road and he decided to go and have a leisurely lunch. It would be the first meal in forty-eight hours he had ordered himself and the thought gave an edge to his appetite.

The restaurant had a delightful little terrace at the back with three tables set out beneath a vine. They were all unoccupied and he chose one in a corner.

A girl came forward and handed him a slate on which the day's menu had been written. At least that was his assumption, but since he was unable to understand a word, it could just as well have been her school home-work. She looked about fifteen and watched him gravely as he glanced at the writing which resembled nothing so much as a tangle of spaghetti.

He handed it back to her with a helpless grin.

'Meat?' she asked.

'Yes, anything you suggest.' She went to move off and he called out, 'Raki,' and made a drinking gesture. She nodded. After two days of enforced abstinence he looked forward to hard alcohol again, though he was not ready for the panto-mime which ensued.

An old man wearing a coarse black apron came forward carrying a tray on which were two glasses, a bottle and a jug of water. He poured the Raki into the smaller glass and with tremendous gusto indicated that Martin should toss it back neat. At the same time he filled the larger glass with water and passed him that as soon as he had downed the Raki.

He seemed content to perpetuate this cycle of action until either Martin or the bottle expired. After the third one, how-ever, Martin held up both hands in an attitude of surrender and the old man padded away with an air of disappointment. It was powerful stuff, and aniseed was something of which he was not particularly fond. If he had realised in advance that the country's national drink bore that flavour, he would un-doubtedly have been less dashing in the first place. The food, which the girl brought him shortly afterwards, helped, how-ever, to stem the more ravaging effects of what he had drunk. It was a delicious stew made up of small, tender pieces of lamb and served with rice and vegetables. He completed his meal with a couple of juicy peaches.

On leaving the restaurant, he went in search of somewhere to lie down and take a siesta, and found a grassy knoll about two hundred yards back from the road. It was quite secluded on its far side and he stretched out with a contented sigh. When he woke up, he must really get down to planning his next move. Not that there was much planning to be done. The Villa Yekta was his only hope, and not much of a hope at that from a preliminary inspection. But it was that or nothing.

As sleep overcame him, he reflected drowsily that, for a man confronted by a forty-eight hours deadline to deliver the goods or suffer very disagreeable consequences, he was behaving with quixotic unconcern. It must be the triple Raki on top of the past four days.

It was four o'clock when he woke up and the sun had dis-appeared behind the hillside. He had already decided that he would try and gain access to the Villa Yekta from the next-door garden and that he would have to wait until after dark before making a move, preferably until around ten or eleven o'clock.

He did not want to show himself where his presence was likely to attract attention, which meant that he had little option but to remain where he was. The only concession he made was to go and sit on the roadside of the knoll from where he could at least watch the lights of ships on the Bosporus about half a mile distant. It was a pleasantly warm evening and the hardship of his self-imposed wait was considerably less than it might have been.

At ten o'clock he made his way down to the road and walked back towards the villa. On reaching it, he clambered once more to his vantage point in the wood on the opposite side of the road to see if any lights were shining from the interior. It appeared that there were none, though a very faint yellow reflection at one of the shuttered windows might have been caused by a light from inside.

He regained the road and, keeping well into the shadow of the hillside, moved to a point where he was opposite the entrance of the next-door villa. It had a wrought-iron gate, which proved, however, to be heavily padlocked when he came to examine it. That, at least, seemed to indicate the villa was unoccupied. Its surrounding wall was also much lower than Villa Yekta's, being no more than six feet.

Though it was a good many years since Martin had had occasion to climb over a wall of that height, he did not feel unduly daunted by the prospect. He walked to the further corner of the property. Then once he saw that no cars were coming from either direction, he stretched up, gripped the top of the wall and with one good heave was over. He landed in some shrubs, which helped to break his fall, but which suffered in the process.

The villa itself was in complete darkness. Nevertheless he was not going to take any risks, and he skirted round the edge of the garden, hugging the wall, which, as he expected, grew another six feet on the Villa Yekta side. He would have to find something to enable him to get over. A search near the house revealed what appeared to be the top of a cucumber frame. He carried it down to the point he had chosen for his climb and propped it against the wall. It would be necessary to take it over with him for his return. He did not imagine he would be able to find any climbing aids on Villa Yekta property.

It was with a sense, first of exhilaration, that he dropped

safely down on the farther side, and then of mounting excitement that he saw lights in two of the ground floor windows. Drawn blinds shone like rectangles of pale parchment.

Keeping close to the wall, he crept up until he was level with the back aspect of the villa, then he darted across to a corner of the building.

The nearest window was only five yards away and he moved towards it with the utmost caution. He scarcely dared breathe as he reached it. At this end, the blind overlapped the edge of the window and to his disappointment he found there was not even a hairline chink through which to peer. Crouching below the level of the window he crawled along to the other end.

The blind was obviously hung at a distorted angle and the overlap at one end meant a gap at the other.

Standing up, he found himself looking into a room lit by a chandelier. There were two chintz covered arm-chairs in the foreground and, over against the far wall, a table.

At the table a man sat playing patience alone.

Martin choked back a quick gasp of surprise, for he recognised the man immediately.

CHAPTER EIGHTEEN

To Peacock, one of the major frustrations of the mid-twentieth century was delay when travelling by air. The fact that it did not happen very often only made it worse on those occasions when one was left to gnawing impatience in some utterly anonymous airport lounge which was not necessarily even on one's route.

On the whole, he enjoyed jet travel, but it always seemed that it was on those journeys which had an element of urgency that he found himself deposited somewhere on the way.

So it was with a jaundiced eye that he looked down on the brilliantly illuminated coast-line of the Sea of Marmara as the Trident came in to land at Yesilköy Airport outside Istanbul. It was after eleven o'clock and they should have landed at six-fifteen. There had been a two hours delay before they even left London, due apparently to an electrical fault, and a further three hours had been spent at Athens while the plane was grimly searched for a bomb. All this had induced a mood of sullen resignation in most of the passengers, not to mention the cabin crew who were going to be done out of an evening in town.

But Peacock had no time for the frustrations of others as he went down the landing steps and walked across to the terminal building. He saw Tillotson waiting just beyond the Customs barrier.

At least his diplomatic passport ensured him the minimum of bother in coping with the arrival formalities.

'Hold-up in Athens, I gather?' Tillotson remarked as he took Peacock's bag from him. 'Car's just outside. Hart's waiting there.'

'Any news of Ainsworth?' Peacock asked urgently. He had arrived and was not disposed to waste time on small talk about his journey. It would not have mattered less if a wing had dropped off. He was now here.

' 'Fraid not . . . Here's the car.' He opened the front passenger's door and Peacock got in, giving Hart an unenthusiastic 'good evening' as Tillotson went round to the driver's side.

'I'm afraid we've still no trace of Ainsworth,' Hart said in a neutral sort of tone.

'So I understand . . .'

'Though we have evidence that he has been moved since he was brought here first. Perhaps Dick had better tell you about it as it comes from one of his contacts.'

Tillotson nodded, gave a wide berth to an airport bus which was pulling away from the kerb and began.

'It seems pretty certain that Ainsworth was held for twenty-four hours or so at an address near the Piyalepasa Mosque. That's in Beyoglu, the bit of town between the Golden Horn and the Bosporus. But the house is now deserted, abandoned in a hurry from all accounts, and it looks as though he was taken elsewhere last night.'

'Why should they have done that?' Peacock asked.

'It seems probable that they're proposing to move him every so often in order to avoid our getting on to them. Gorsev is a wily fellow and he realises very well what Ainsworth represents.'

'How does Gorsev manage to have so many hide-outs at his disposal?'

'That's not difficult in this city.'

'No, I suppose not,' Peacock said quietly. He wished his

question had not sounded so petulant. It was a sign of weakness as much as of tension. 'Are you still in touch with Gorsev?'

'After a day of silence, he made contact again this evening. As a matter of fact, I feel there's something a bit odd going on, but I can't make out what. Brian and I were discussing it on our way out to the airport this evening.'

'Odd in what way?'

'Gorsev's earlier contact with me was through a couple of intermediaries, but then quite suddenly he, so to speak, went off the air. He just vanished and no one knew where he was. But about eight o'clock this evening he phoned me and ... well, he sounded pretty agitated.' Tillotson paused and it was Hart who spoke.

'Dangerously agitated from what you told me, Dick.'

'He was jittery all right. He said that if the swap didn't go through by six o'clock tomorrow evening, the deal was off. That Ainsworth would suffer and that he would ensure we got the dirty end of the stick publicity-wise.'

'Do you believe him?'

'I don't think they'll kill Ainsworth,' Tillotson said dispassionately. 'If only because he's a much better asset alive than dead. In fact his corpse would be no asset at all.'

'But if they decided to cut their losses, mightn't they kill him in those circumstances?'

'It's possible, but I still doubt it,' Hart put in.

'The one thing which must at all costs be avoided is publicity involving our use of Ainsworth. You remember what happened over Crabbe? If it ever got out that we induced a highly respected member of the Bar to help us on a job, as a result of which he ended up dead or in the dock on a state spy trial, we could all hand in our resignations and retire to the South Pacific.' He paused. 'Well, *I* have to, anyway.'

'But presumably Ainsworth agreed to help us with his eyes open?' Hart said vigorously.

'Oh yes, I told him there were minimal dangers,' Peacock said wearily. 'But it's the fact of his being kidnapped and held to ransom which puts it in a very different light. If we're prepared to pay the price, Ainsworth will be returned in one piece. If we're not, then, metaphorically if not literally speaking, the spotlight is going to be turned on his mangled remains for all the world to see, and that includes the British public. That's where the bite is in the present situation. It's the fact that we can rescue him, *at a price.*'

'And you're suggesting that we may have to pay the price?' Hart asked disbelievingly. He had spent months planning this operation under Peacock's supervision. It had succeeded in the face of numerous hazards and here was Peacock proposing that they might have to yield up their hard-won prize.

'Yes.'

'It'll mean that no one will dare defect again in a hundred years,' Hart observed bitterly. 'We get someone out from behind the curtain and then hand him back again. Quite frankly, it's unthinkable.'

'So is the other alternative,' Peacock replied firmly. Silence fell for two or three minutes while each contemplated the unpalatable truths which confronted them. It was Peacock who broke it. 'Perhaps there'll be further news when we get to your office, Dick,' he said. 'Meanwhile fill me in on some of the other details.' He twisted round so that he could see Hart. 'You were right about Anna Schmidt, it seems?'

'Yes, the little bitch! I'd been fairly certain for some time she was a double. There'd been a couple of leaks and everything pointed to her as being responsible. When this operation came up, it seemed a good opportunity of putting my suspicions to the test. In the event, she obviously spilled all she knew to the other side, with the result that the Bulgarians were ready and waiting.'

'What story did she actually give them?' Tillotson asked.

'The cover story I gave her was that an East German woman named Paula Zwehl was the object of rescue and that we had devised a plan for getting her out which necessitated a decoy operation. I told Anna that she had been picked for a part in the decoy operation since she had a physical resemblance to Paula Zwehl. Quite simply all she had to do was, at a given point—in fact the morning the bus left Sofia—to alter her appearance slightly so that it would be thought that she had been replaced on the bus by Paula Zwehl. I told her that it would be leaked to the other side what was going to happen so that their attention would be focused on the bus while Paula Zwehl was spirited out by other means. Of course, Anna Schmidt immediately passed the whole story to the other side herself, with the result that the unfortunate Paula Zwehl was arrested and, for all I know, is still in a cell at Security Police headquarters in Sofia.'

'There really is a Paula Zwehl then?'

'Certainly. She's a secretary to some high-up in the East German Ministry of State Security. She was going to be in Sofia as a member of the same delegation as Vlastov. It was he who supplied us with all the necessary details to enable us to work out a plan.'

'Was Ainsworth given the same story as Anna Schmidt?' Tillotson inquired.

'Not quite,' Peacock said. 'He knew nothing about a decoy plan. He thought that Anna Schmidt was going to be replaced on the bus by Paula Zwehl who resembled her.'

Tillotson smiled. 'So Anna Schmidt is told one thing and Ainsworth another, while a third is successfully executed.'

'It had to be, particularly as it had a dual purpose, the rescue of Vlastov and the confirmation of our suspicions about Anna Schmidt.'

'No wonder the Bulgarians and the East Germans are hopping mad. All they've done is arrest an innocent woman.'

'They were pretty clumsy, too,' Hart said. 'Hans tells me that the woman they planted on the bus and who pretended to be Paula Zwehl was a real ham.'

'What happened to her?' Peacock asked.

'She was left drugged in a ditch.' Hart gave a mirthless chuckle. 'I must say one can almost feel sorry for Ainsworth. As far as he was concerned, the whole thing went disastrously wrong from the moment Anna Schmidt defected. He immediately came under grave suspicion, though luckily she was unable to tell them more than that he was on the bus in the rôle of silent escort; then he was interrogated; then the ersatz Paula Zwehl pops up next to him ... He really must have thought he was in some James Bond hell.'

'Not to mention what has happened to him subsequently,' Peacock said grimly.

This observation brought them back to what was uppermost in all their minds. Ainsworth or Vlastov? That was soon, it seemed, to be the agonising choice.

'Where is Vlastov by the way?' he asked.

'At the Villa Yekta,' Tillotson replied, and then added, 'No chance of his being discovered there.'

CHAPTER NINETEEN

It was a few minutes after midnight when Martin arrived back in the city.

He had found a taxi parked outside a café not far from the Villa Yekta and, with less difficulty than he had expected, had persuaded the driver to take him back to Istanbul. He had had to wait while the man drank his beer and to agree an exaggerated, but not outrageous, fare for the trip.

The taxi put him down at the Sirkeci Station and he immediately phoned Mr Gursan at the number he had been given.

It seemed at first that no one had ever heard of the name of Gursan, but eventually he was put through to someone who told him in fractured English that a car would pick him up in ten minutes time.

He went outside and stood where he had been told to wait. He felt tremendously elated by his success at the villa. Admittedly it had been his only hope, but it had also been a forlorn one. He still did not pretend to understand all that had happened, though it was abundantly plain that Peacock had wilfully deceived him. He would doubtless justify that on the need-to-know principle, but so far as Martin was concerned it removed any lingering scruples he may have had about passing his discovery on to Mr Gursan.

Knowing Peacock, he probably never would be told all the details of the operation in which he had been assigned a walking-on part. That there had been a decoy plan of some sort was now apparent, but he could only begin to guess at parts of it. Anna Schmidt's sudden disappearance, for example, still remained an unsolved mystery in his mind. However, it had finally been borne in on him that the operation as a whole had succeeded and not been the perilous fiasco he had believed. Perilous, yes; fiasco, apparently not.

It was with a certain satisfaction that he decided there would be no need to tell Peacock of his visit to the Villa Yekta, when they met again. The need-to-know principle was of two way application.

He had no doubt that a debriefing session awaited him, they would be particularly anxious to learn all they could about his lost hours: lost days, indeed—and he would have to decide

147

how much he was prepared to tell.

As he stood there watching the cars and taxis hurtle round a bend on their approach to the Galata Bridge, he realised that the only sense of obligation he felt, arising from the whole affair, was towards Heck and Rache.

Late though it was, the night was full of noise and movement. Neon flickered erratically and new sodium street lighting covered a nearby area with hideous clarity.

But this was a city which was alive. Its winding alleys might conceal untold squalor, but compared with staid Sofia it throbbed with life.

A voice spoke behind him.

'Come, car.'

He swung round to see the young man to whom Mr Gursan had handed him over the previous night.

To Martin's surprise they did not cross the Galata Bridge and make for the building in Beyoglu where he had originally been taken. Instead, they soon drew up outside an ordinary police station close by the Golden Horn. It resembled one of London's more Dickensian corrective institutions and Martin's nose was assailed by a number of powerful smells, which fought for supremacy as they entered. He was taken upstairs and into a tiny room. Behind a table covered with tattered files sat Mr Gursan. He pointed at the only other chair in the room.

'You have come to tell me what I required you to find out?'

'Yes.'

'Good. You have done well. I thought it would take you longer.' To Martin's surprise he pulled out a very English looking pipe, peered dubiously into the bowl and then lit it. For a second he all but disappeared behind a cloud of smoke. Leaning forward, he said, 'I am listening.'

'Before I tell you what I've found out, may we confirm your side of the bargain? In exchange for the information, you will release Heckstrap and Miss Lingman and you will not place any obstacles in the way of my departure?'

A flash of anger passed through Mr Gursan's eyes. Martin had not wished to rile him, though he had foreseen the possibility. On the other hand, his lawyer's training required him to reiterate the terms of the bargain before disclosing his hand.

'I have given my word,' he said stiffly. 'I am able to keep it as well as any Englishman.'

'That I'm sure of,' Martin said hastily.

'But my side of the bargain depends on what you tell me.'

'I am ready to tell you now.'

Mr Gursan's lips parted slightly in an expression of animal satisfaction.

'It is not a name...'

Mr Gursan started up in anger again.

'If you are fooling me, it will be very bad for you and your friends.'

'I'd have hardly got in touch if my intention was to fool you. Now, would I?'

'Go on.'

'The man who was smuggled out of Bulgaria was the man dressed as a guard, who held the bus up just before the frontier and who took off the girl sitting next to me.' Martin was relieved to observe Mr Gursan's absorbed expression. 'I am unable to tell you his name, but I have given you the most important part.'

There was a silence before Mr Gursan spoke. 'How do you know this?'

'I have seen the man and I recognised him.'

'Where?'

Martin smiled wryly. 'That wasn't part of the bargain,' he said quietly.

'How do I know you are telling the truth? How can I check the information?'

'In the first place, it makes sense, doesn't it?'

'Many things you could tell me would make sense. No, it is not enough, I must know where you saw this man.'

Martin bit his lip. He thought that Mr Gursan probably did believe him. If only he could offer him a piece of corroboration without disclosing the use of the Villa Yekta by the Intelligence Service of his own country. That he was not prepared to do.

The door suddenly opened and the young man who had fetched him from the station came in. He and Mr Gursan spoke for a minute and then Mr Gursan left the room abruptly. The young man remained standing against the door to deter any thoughts of departure Martin might be entertaining.

It was over half an hour before Mr Gursan returned. For Martin it was an anxious half-hour. His earlier sense of elation had given way to alternating moods of despair and apathetic resignation.

149

'You are lucky,' Mr Gursan said as he sat down again. 'I have been able to confirm what you've told me. One of Gorsev's men has been persuaded to talk. He was picked up less than half an hour ago. The man you saw is one Ernst Vlastov, an East German of Bulgarian origin, who was a senior official in the Ministry of Defence in Berlin.' A grin broke slowly across his face. 'It seems, my friend, that Gorsev is still pretending to your people that you are in his custody. He is like the man who hopes no one will notice that his trousers have fallen down.' He rose. 'I am ready to abide by our bargain. If I may give you some advice, it is that you should leave Istanbul as soon as possible. It is a dangerous place for you to linger in. As for Mr Vlastov, I hope your people will remove him soon, as well. Perhaps if we pretend to look the other way, they will feel bold enough to spirit him away to England. This is not a difficult city for people such as he to be got away from. So many ships of all nationalities ... It both makes my job easier and more difficult.' He looked at his watch. 'Where will you stop tonight?'

'Can I stay here till morning?'

Mr Gursan shrugged. 'It is not often that someone wishes to stop at one of our police stations, but it is permitted in the circumstances.'

Martin now fixed him with a quizzical look. There were still a couple of matters about which he wanted to satisfy his curiosity.

'Would I be right in thinking it was you who tried my bedroom door at the hotel in Zagreb?'

'You were not in the dining-room at dinner and I wondered where you were. My nose told me that perhaps you were already up to something ... I had to be suspicious of everyone.'

Martin nodded. 'Speaking of suspicion, were any of the other passengers involved in this game among the shadows?'

'No.'

'I had thought the Springers might...'

'Ah! I, too, wondered about that couple. Dr Springer, I discover, is a Byzantine scholar. He is very rich, but very mean. Frau Springer is his fourth wife. She is also his secretary and speaks many languages.' Mr Gursan pulled a face. 'She has lived, that one! Perhaps she will be lucky and he will not survive too long.'

'She'll probably find he has left all his money to further

Byzantine scholarship.'

'She is not stupid,' Mr Gursan observed severely.

'And Fräulein Benzl? I wondered about her, too.'

'A schoolteacher. What else?'

'She did rather look like one. Almost too much so!'

Mr Gursan was showing signs of wishing to bring the conversation to an end.

'There is one last thing,' Martin said, 'I should like to see Heckstrap and Miss Lingman before I leave Istanbul.'

'They are here.'

'At this station?'

'I had them brought here tonight. They will be released in the morning.'

'And their car?'

'That is up to them. I am not yet running a garage.'

Five minutes later, Martin was having a reunion with Heck and Rache in an indescribably filthy cell in the basement of the building.

They were stretched out side by side on a narrow wooden shelf, which served as a bed.

'Hello, look who's here!' Rache said, as the cell door was opened to admit Martin. 'The cause of all our troubles.'

She spoke without rancour, but Martin was going to feel embarrassed whatever either of them said.

'I'm afraid I can't make full amends,' he said awkwardly, 'but at least I can tell you that you're going to be released in the morning.'

'Hear that, Heck? He says we're going to be released.'

Heck swung his legs off the shelf and sat up.

'You a friend of the chief of police or something?' he asked. 'Doesn't matter if you are. We don't mind being let out as a result of a spot of corruption.'

'*We do not*,' Rache said emphatically. 'I can do without Turkish prisons.'

'You'll find they get worse as we go farther east,' Heck remarked.

'You're still bound for India then?' Martin asked.

'We might as well go there as anywhere.'

'You're talking like an uncommitted worm,' Rache broke in. 'Of course we're still going to India.'

'And the car?'

'We may have to abandon that,' Heck said vaguely. 'Rache wants to buy a couple of horses.'

'That's right. And we can trade them in for a camel when we get to a desert.'

Martin stood there marvelling. He could only hope that providence would continue to watch over them, though he thought it was going to be a full time job.

'I'm flying back to England tomorrow,' he said. 'I shan't have further need of my foreign currency. I've got quite a bit here, mostly Swiss francs. Will you take it, please? It'll help to buy a camel.' It gave him considerable satisfaction to reflect that Peacock's secretly manipulated funds would in due course have to absorb this hidden disbursement.

Heck took the money and put it in his hip pocket without bothering to look at it.

'If you insist,' he said with a grin. 'Move yourself, woman, I want to try and get some sleep.'

'Well, I'm going on the inside this time, so you move your great backside,' Rache retorted.

Martin left them to their rest.

He spent the remainder of the night in the tiny room in which he had been interviewed, sitting up on a hard chair.

In a few hours time, he would take a taxi to the Herold Touring office.

He looked forward to seeing their faces when he walked in to claim his baggage as though nothing had happened...

》》 If you've enjoyed this book and would like to discover more great vintage crime and thriller titles, as well as the most exciting crime and thriller authors writing today, visit: 》》

The Murder Room
Where Criminal Minds Meet

themurderroom.com

www.ingramcontent.com/pod-product-compliance
Ingram Content Group UK Ltd.
Pitfield, Milton Keynes, MK11 3LW, UK
UKHW040436280225
455666UK00003B/115